Brooklyn on Lock 2

Sonovia Alexander

Lock Down Publications
Presents
Brooklyn on Lock 2
A Novel by *Sonovia Alexander*

Sonovia Alexander

Lock Down Publications
P.O. Box 1482
Pine Lake, Ga 30072-1482

Lock Down Publications
Like our page on Facebook: Lock Down Publications @www.facebook.com/lockdownpublications.ldp
Cover design and layout by: Dynasty's Cover Me
Book interior design by: Shawn Walker
Edited by: Mia Rucker

This book is dedicated to each of my supporters.
Thank you!

Sonovia Alexander

Prologue

The Shop
May 17, 2005
Early evening...

Mo sat in the back seat of the truck they were riding in as the driver, Pablo, pressed on the gas pedal speeding down the two way street. He was ordered by his boss to make it to the shop in less than twenty minutes. Pablo ran every red light to keep from going over his time limit.

Mo looked around as they passed different parts of Brooklyn. He hated this place with a passion. Glancing over at T Ski, Mo wondered what was going through his mind. T Ski looked as if he didn't have a care in the world. He could feel Mo's eyes burning a hole in the side of his face but he paid it no mind.

As Pablo came to a complete stop, he hopped out of the car, leaving the car running, and headed inside what looked like a junk yard. Pablo entered through the gates and moved about in a fast pace toward the back until he was no longer seen. Mo turned his attention to his brother.

"Are you going to talk to me or are you going to keep me in the dark? Why are we at a junk yard?" Mo questioned as he shifted his body, leaning back on the car door to get a better look at T Ski.

"I have business here. Pablo had to go retrieve what belongs to me." T Ski glanced at his watch.

"What the fuck do you need me for if you're going to keep dodging my questions? I don't have time for these games man. What the fuck are you doing?" Mo was tired of the games and was ready to walk away from all the bullshit T Ski had him entangled in.

"Bro, it's going to take me too long to explain everything to you. If you watch how I move, the answers will come to you without me revealing them to you. You're not watching the set up close enough. I'm bigger than what you think, Mo," T Ski announced. He didn't feel the need to explain himself but knew that he would have to give his brother a little taste of what he had going on in order for him to keep riding with him.

"I think this is bullshit. You should just go your ass to school and invent something that will make you a shit load of money to get out the fucking hood. All this taking over Brooklyn shit is not worth us losing our lives over. I don't even know how I let you talk me in to going along with this. You are too smart to be thinking so small. Use your abilities for something useful." Mo was having second thoughts. He had Bella on his mind along with his son. He worried about what was going on with Bella and if she was mad at him. It was starting to take a toll on him.

"Mo, geniuses are everywhere. I believe a variety of factors, such as being able to afford education, mingling with the right crowd, where you grew up, and self-perception, play as much of a role in how your life unfolds as your reasoning and computational abilities," T Ski explained. Mo looked at his brother with a raised brow.

"I hear you talking but you're still not making any sense. Your computational thinking can be used to solve problems and can be used efficiently. Don't forget I went to college too. I don't care what your damn IQ is. I understand the ways of life, but I still believe that you can make a drastic change in the world by using your gift with more efficiency," Mo retorted.

"Do you think for one second America would believe that a young boy from the ghetto would be able to make a difference in their lives? They don't give a fuck about my IQ. I have a plan and I know it's going to work." Before T Ski could continue his conversation, Pablo opened the trunk of the car, tossing a big black duffle back inside. He closed the trunk back and headed over to the driver side. Pablo entered the vehicle. Mo wanted to continue their conversation but knew that it would have to wait. Mo didn't trust talking in front of Pablo.

"Where are we headed to now boss?" Pablo asked.

"Take me home. We'll have to take care of everything else first thing in the morning. I have too much to get done in too little time," T Ski explained.

Chapter 1

May 18, 2005

The following morning...

T Ski had awakened Mo at six o'clock the next morning. The sun hadn't even come up yet. T Ski had been up since 1am. He took his shower and was dressed in black Levi jeans and a throw over polo shirt. He wore his timberland boots to complete his outfit. His dreads were neatly tossed to the back of his head in a tight ponytail. He had checked on his mother, awakening Evelyn from her sleep to give her some of the meds he had invented, which were helping her get better.

T Ski had no time to waste. There was too much that he had to get accomplished before the day was over. T Ski knew that his time was limited. He had made sure to remove all of his belongings from his room throughout the course of the night. He wanted to make sure that no one would ask him any questions. T Ski knew that things were about to get hot for him. Although no one but his brother's new that he was behind everything, he was questioning Taz B's loyalty. He didn't believe that his brother would blow him up, but he knew that if Taz was put in an awkward position, he would tell all. T Ski couldn't chance that.

He was moving quicker than he wanted to because he knew that time wasn't on his side.

"We need to get out of here now," T Ski said to Mo. Mo sat up in bed and rubbed the sleep from his eyes.

"Can I at least wash my face and brush my damn teeth?" Mo asked. T Ski didn't respond. He instead walked out of the room and headed toward the kitchen. Mo looked on the side of the bed where Xavier was sound asleep. He kissed his son on the cheek before getting out of the bed.

Mo pulled on the pants he had worn the night before and a t-shirt before walking out of his room heading toward the bathroom. After he took care of his hygiene, Mo put on his sneakers and was ready to go.

"I already spoke with Andrea. She will keep watch over Xavier. Pablo is waiting for us outside, so we need to go now," T Ski explained while looking through his phone.

"I'm ready," Mo stated. Both guys exited the apartment and headed toward the stairs. Mo didn't know what they were going to do today but he hoped that he would be able to talk more with T Ski about his plans.

***

Pablo pulled up in front of a bank. He turned the ignition off and exited the vehicle. Pablo fixed his suit jacket while walking around to the back of the car to open the door for T Ski and Mo. Mo was the first one to exit the vehicle with T Ski following suit. T Ski started off walking toward the entrance with Mo following closely behind. T Ski walked toward the back where only personnel was allowed. Mo didn't question T Ski but was curious to know how he had access to getting through the door where only employees were allowed. Security gave a head nod in T Ski's direction. Mo took note of that and wondered who they were here to see. T Ski knocked on the door that was to the right side upon entering through the main entrance leading back to the offices.

"Come in," Regina said. T Ski opened the door and entered with Mo walking alongside him. Mo had forgotten his aunt worked at the bank. He walked around the desk and gave his aunt a hug and kiss on the cheek. He didn't realize which bank they were at until seeing his aunt.

"How are you, Aunt Regina?" Mo said as he took a seat beside T Ski on the other side of her desk.

"I'm doing well, nephew. Haven't seen you in a while. You look good," Regina said smiling at how handsome both her nephews were.

"Thanks," Mo said as he returned the smile.

"Is everything ready?" T Ski asked as he waited for the two of them to get over their formalities. He had things to do and his aunt knew that his time was limited.

"Yes. Ready for pickup in the next twenty minutes," Regina replied. Mo looked from his aunt back to T Ski, wondering what they were talking about.

"Is the money forwarded?" T Ski questioned.

"Yes. Everything is straight. Do you need a car sent to pick him up or are you going to pick him up yourself?" Regina asked.

"I got it. Hit up Mr. Shaw and set that meeting up for tomorrow morning. I should have everything ready by then," T Ski said as he stood from his seat. Mo was confused. They had just gotten there. He hadn't seen his aunt in a few months. He thought they would at least mingle a bit.

"We're leaving already?" Mo questioned.

"Yes. I have things to do," T Ski replied as he made his way toward the door.

Mo stood up from his seat and followed T Ski. He turned back and waved to his aunt. Mo hated not knowing what was going on. He was definitely going to question T Ski once they made it out of the bank. Mo wasn't feeling all this secrecy shit going on and, if he was going to be a part of what T Ski had planned, he didn't need any surprises.

T Ski reached outside the bank with Mo behind him. His phone started ringing. T Ski pulled it out of his pocket and looked at the caller ID. He pressed the talk button and answered.

"Hello. Yes. When? I'll be there shortly. Who's there? Okay thanks," T Ski said as he ended the call and placed his phone back inside of his pocket.

"Where are we heading now?" Mo questioned.

"We are heading to Downstate hospital to see Bella," T Ski replied as he walked off, heading toward the car. Mo could feel his anger arising again. He tried so hard to contain himself but he couldn't understand for the life of him why T Ski knew where his woman was and he didn't. Why a phone call came to T-Ski's phone and not his. Mo wasn't feeling the idea of being left in the dark when it had something to do with the woman he loved and shared a child with. Mo entered the car and closed the door behind him. He wanted answers.

"Do you want to share with me why someone is contacting you about my baby mother?" Mo questioned, staring at T Ski.

"I have connections," T Ski responded dryly. He wasn't in the mood to sit there and explain things to his brother. He was pushing for time and had moves to make.

"This car is not moving until you tell me what the fuck is going on. Bella's parents made it clear to me that they were going to keep me from her and they had moved her from the hospital she was in. Now you, on the other hand, know which hospital she's in and receiving phone calls about her. That shit is not sitting well with me, bro. You are going to have to tell me more than just you having fucking connection,s" Mo said with an attitude.

"I keep watch over all of my family. I knew the hospital that she was transferred to before she was transferred there. Her parents think that they are controlling things but they're not. I told you not to worry about it. Her folks don't have the money to pay any of her medical expenses, so they don't really have a say in the matter concerning her. I have someone I have to pick up in a few, so we need to make this quick. Please let Pablo get us to the hospital so you can see your woman and then I can make my way to handle my business," T Ski responded.

Mo shook his head. He leaned back in the seat without saying another word. He was somewhat happy that he would finally get to see Bella to see her progress.

T Ski pulled out his cell phone and sent a mass text to a few people. Mo tried to look over to see what he was texting, but didn't have much luck.

"Do you plan on going to college and getting a degree in something?" Mo questioned, breaking the silence between the two of them.

"I have that worked out," T Ski replied. His answers were short and simple.

Mo wondered what kind of man his brother was turning into. This was not the T Ski that he had watched grow up. It felt like Mo was sitting next to a total stranger. Here it was his baby brother was bringing in thousands of dollars and calling all the shots while he sat back taking orders and waiting for the next move. Mo couldn't believe how things were changing in such a short timeframe. T Ski was getting niggas killed and set up without getting his hands or name involved. No one knew that a teenage boy was behind all that was going down in the hood. Mo worried about what would happen if this shit blew up in their face. He hoped that Bella was well enough and would be home to look after their son. He couldn't bring himself to think that some strangers would have his son's future in the palm of their hands. He couldn't let that happen.

A short while later, Pablo pulled into the parking lot of the hospital. Mo and T Ski both exited the car and headed toward the main entrance of the hospital. T Ski walked toward the security guard and whispered something to him. The security guard looked over at Mo and then nodded his head for them both to follow him. Mo shook his head. He knew that his brother had pull but he wondered how and who he knew that he could just walk into certain places, whisper something in someone's ear, and they do what he asked of them. Mo wasn't feeling jaundiced, but just wanted to know what was so special about his brother to have people cater to him the way that they did.

Chapter 2

Riverdale Projects

"What are you doing here, ma?" Tadow asked Sheryl as she walked into the apartment.

"I want to know what's going on with you and your brother. There was some guys that came to my apartment looking for the both of you. Now I know that the two of you have better sense than to be out here doing things you have no business doing and having people knocking on my door looking for you. Thank God your father was home and scared these men off," Sheryl explained.

"What did they look like, ma?" Tadow asked with an attitude. He was going to kill whoever it was that had balls enough to show up at his mom's crib. That was the ultimate no-no. Whatever score niggas had to settle with him should be with him. Now niggas were going to feel his rage.

"It doesn't matter what they look like. Why would anyone be out looking for you and Lee? What the hell are the both of you into now? You know who your father is. How could you guys be that stupid?" Sheryl questioned.

"Ma, I don't know what you're thinking but we're not doing anything. But I know I'm going to find out who it was that came to your house looking for me and handle that shit. Niggas crossed the line when they step to family. I don't know why niggas is looking for me or Lee. We have been chilling for a minute. Why did you come all the way over here by yourself knowing that you were already approached by some fools? I don't want you walking the streets alone, mama," Tadow said. He was trying his best to hold in his anger. He was about to call his brother and get shit popping, once he found out who the niggas were.

"I'm not going to be afraid to walk these streets that I lived in for all of these years. I was on my way to go and see your aunt. Once I leave here, that's where I'm going but I had to come and find out what you and Lee were involved in to have so many men coming to my house for you. It was about seven of them. Once they saw your father's badge, they backed away without another word. I don't like worrying about you boys. You guys are both grown and make your own choices but when it starts affecting me then that becomes a problem. Your father is a commissioner and while coming to pick me up, this is what happens. This isn't sitting too well with him, you know. I don't need you boys out there embarrassing him. He wanted long ago for us to leave

Brooklyn because of something like this happening but I talked him into staying here because of all of our family. I regret the day that I didn't leave Brooklyn. Now look what's happening," Sheryl retorted.

"Don't worry about this, ma. I'm going to handle things. Let me walk you over to Aunt Evelyn's house. Give me a minute," Tadow said as he started off toward his bedroom to retrieve his gun.

Sheryl looked around her son's apartment and shook her head. She knew that Tadow and Lee were drug dealers. There was no way that they could afford all the expensive things they had in the apartment working as a security guard. At least that's what they told their mother they did for a living. Sheryl didn't get involved in her sons' business because they were grown men and were going to live their lives the way they wanted to anyway. She didn't see the purpose in trying to get them to change. Their father was above law enforcement and she couldn't understand how they could choose to become drug dealers knowing the hard work their father put in everyday overseeing the law that put people like them in prison. He worked closely with the government and didn't need his sons embarrassing him. Perry had done everything he could to be a provider for his wife and kids and to make sure that his sons had a good example to follow. Sheryl couldn't understand why her sons chose the path they did instead of becoming successful.

Tadow walked back into the living room. "You ready to go, ma?" he asked as he adjusted his clothing so his mother couldn't see his gun print. Sheryl shook her head.

"I don't want to be walking with you if you have a weapon on you. If you are in any kind of trouble, you need to stay your ass in this house until you find out what's going on. I don't want to see anything happen to you out here in these streets, boy, but you and your brother have hard heads. I don't know what made you both want to be out here hustling. You had a good upbringing and I just can't see why you would want to throw your lives away for fast money. Everyone knows what happens to drug dealers. Rather you wind up in jail or dead. There's only two choices in this lifestyle you're living. You obviously don't care," Sheryl explained.

"I do care whether I live or die, ma. I told you that I'm not out here hustling. I don't understand why you keep assuming that I do," Tadow said.

"Those men weren't at my house to say hello or to see how you were doing. They came there like you owed them something.

I said what I had to say to you. I don't want you following behind me with that gun in your pocket, so you can stay right on inside this house. I will manage to make it to my sister's house just fine by myself, like I made it here alone," Sheryl explained as she opened the front door and proceeded out of the apartment towards the elevator.

Tadow shook his head. He held the door open and took his gun out of his pocket and placed it on the table. He didn't feel comfortable letting his mother walk the streets alone after telling him that someone had paid her a visit. Sheryl didn't know that Tadow had another gun in the small of his back. He showed her the gun he took out of his pocket just so she would allow him to walk with her, thinking that he was unarmed. Tadow wasn't stepping foot out of his door without protection.

***

Downstate Hospital

Mo gave Bella's name at the front desk and was given a pass to her room. Mo was given a different name to use in order to be able to visit with Bella. Her parents had noted that he was not allowed to visit her. Mo prayed that her parents weren't up visiting her because he knew they wouldn't permit him in to see her. He didn't want to cause a scene at the hospital and be carried out in handcuffs if revoked. Mo just wanted to make sure that his girl was doing okay. He wasn't looking for trouble. He had enough on his mind as it was.

Mo and T Ski rode the elevator to the floor Bella's room was on. Mo was nervous because he didn't know what to expect. He looked over in T Ski's direction and saw how calm his brother was. He didn't have a care in the world. It bothered Mo a bit but he didn't say anything.

They walked in the direction of Bella's room together and, when they reached the door, T Ski let Mo walk ahead of him to give him and Bella their privacy. T Ski decided to go over to the waiting area and have a seat. Mo watched his brother pass by the room and go to the waiting area as he took a deep breath in and walked into Bella's room. She was up and alert. Mo was shocked to see her looking like herself. He didn't expect her to be coherent, being that the last time he saw her, she was in bad condition.

"Hey, how are you feeling?" Mo asked as he walked over to Bella's bed and stood by her. Bella looked at Mo with a look of death. Mo was confused and didn't know what that was about.

"What the hell are you doing here? I don't want to see you. Where is my son? I don't want him around you or your crazy ass family. I want you to get the hell out of here right now before I call the police on you," Bella shouted.

Mo didn't know what the hell was going on with Bella and why she was treating him this way. He was confused and thought that she had too much medication that was messing with her thinking process because he hadn't done any wrong to her to be talked to like this.

"What's going on with you, Bella? What did I do to you? Are you really going to get me locked up? I wanted to make sure that you were good. What's with the attitude?" Mo questioned.

"Get out of here, Mo. I don't ever want to see you as long as I live. I hate you and your deranged ass family. You're all crazy," Bella continued to shout. She didn't care who heard her. She was pissed off.

"What the fuck do my family have to do with anything? I'll leave if that's what you want but I'm not giving anyone my son but you. When you get out of here, you know where to find me," Mo said.

"You will never see my son again. When I get out tomorrow, I'm coming to get my son and we are out of here. I don't want him around you," Bella said. Bella started to say something else when she saw T Ski pass by her room. He glanced at her and made eye contact for a brief second before he kept walking. "Please leave Mo," Bella asked in a much calmer tone.

Mo shook his head and proceeded out of her room. Two nurses were on their way into Bella's room, after hearing her shouting. They wanted to make sure that she was okay.

"I don't know what the hell is going on with her and why she was talking to me like that. She's talking about the family as if one of us are the cause of her being here. Do you know what's wrong with her, since you seem to know everything else? I want to know how she is being released from the hospital so early if she was shot. I don't understand any of this," Mo asked T Ski with an attitude.

T Ski shook his head and moved toward the elevator.

"Wasn't you just in the waiting area?" Mo questioned.

"I was in the waiting area. I have somewhere I need to be in a few. I need to get up to Rikers Island," T Ski said.

Mo couldn't believe this shit. It took everything he had in him not to knock his little brother out because he didn't like how T Ski was just brushing everything off like it wasn't nothing. Mo didn't know what the hell was going on with his baby's mother and all this little nigga could think about was having him run around with him to different places.

"T Ski, is there something that you know that I don't. You sitting here like you don't give a fuck about what I'm going through. I know you clearly just heard what the fuck was said back there. What the fuck is going on?" Mo said, raising his voice.

"We can talk when we get in the car. Let's just hurry up and get out of here." T Ski said calmly.

Mo pressed the button to the elevator and couldn't help but stare at his brother. Shit was becoming a bit much for Mo and he didn't know how long he was going to be able to hold his composure. He felt like he was losing control over his life. Mo thought about what Bella said when she threatened him by saying he would never see his son again. That shit irked the hell out of him. He would kill that bitch first before he let her take his son out of his life when he took care of his child. Bella really was on something if she thought he was going to let that happen. Mo felt like packing his son up and just leaving town, but knew that he couldn't leave his mother behind. Mo wanted to explode. He didn't want to lose it, but he started feeling like he was going to go crazy.

The elevator opened. Mo and T Ski stepped on and rode to the first floor. T Ski's phone started going off. He pulled his phone out of his pocket.

"Hello," T Ski answered. "I'm not around. Give me two hours top. Thanks." T Ski disconnected the call and placed his phone back into his pocket. The elevator doors opened and T Ski was first to step off and start for the exit.

Mo was lost in his thoughts. He had so many things running through his mind right now. He was contemplating on how he would be able to get his son out of Brooklyn but still make sure that his mother was okay. Mo knew that it would be impossible to just up and leave after what had been taking place in the last few days. He also had to worry about Andrea's wellbeing as well, since she was still home.

T Ski's phone went off again as they both entered the vehicle. Mo shook his head, knowing that he wasn't going to get anything out of T Ski at this point.

Mo waited until T Ski was done with his call before speaking. "Have your driver drop me back to the house. I'm sure you can handle your business alone. I have went to all these locations with you and still don't know what the fuck is going on. I need to be home seeing about my son."

T Ski didn't say anything in response to what Mo shared.

"Pablo, drop my brother off before taking me to my next destination," T Ski said.

Mo closed his eyes and said a silent prayer for God to keep him from choking the life out of his brother. He didn't like this new attitude that T Ski possessed. It was cold and unloving.

***

Seth Low Projects

"What's good on the streets, Dogg?" Ace said as he sipped on his Hennessey.

"I'm chilling, homey. I got some shit that I need you to move with me but I need to make sure this shit is right. I been trying to holla at your ass all damn week but I know you busy. I just came through to check on you, though, to make sure you good," Dogg said.

"I'm good, son. I need to get my hands on some more work. I got cats across the building that is starving. That nigga El Boogie been dodging my calls for a few days. I'm busted," Ace explained.

"I got you my nigga. Give me until the weekend but I need for you and your squad to be ready to hit up some niggas. The shit I got in mind is going to put us all on top. I need niggas to be sure if they can handle this shit. We gon have to knock some niggas off the map," Dogg remarked.

"We always ready and will pop anytime. I just need to make sure that you're going to come through and make sure that all our pockets get right. I got some hitters on Sutter Ave too, if I need to get them on board," Ace replied.

"That's what I'm talking about. I'll be back over here to rap with you tomorrow. I got some shit to handle but I got you, fam. Shit bout to get live," Dogg was excited. He was glad that Ace was coming on board with him. He needed ruthless niggas on his team for what he had in mind.

"That's a good look, son. I will hit the rest of these niggas up and let them know that we will be back in business."

"Yea, you do that. I'll holla at you later," Dogg said as he walked off from Ace. He knew there was money to be made over here and he wanted to dominate this side of Brownsville before niggas started moving in.

Ace was glad that he had ran into Dogg. He was hearing good things about his childhood friend. Ace was looking to get his hand on some work. He worked for El Boogie, but no one had heard from him in a few days. Word around the hood was that El Boogie had saved up all his dough and left town without saying a word. Ace hoped that it wasn't true because he had a family to take care of. Getting a job wouldn't be easy for a nigga like Ace being that he was only twenty-six years old with three felonies. No one was quick to give a nigga like him a job.

Ace was tempted to go on the other side and get down with those new cats everyone had been talking about. He was trying to give El Boogie the benefit of the doubt, hoping that the nigga might've gotten knocked by the cops instead of thinking he left town without supplying his team with his connections. Ace hoped that Dogg came through for them.

Sonovia Alexander

Chapter 3

Marcus Garvey Projects

"Yo, this nigga tried to front on me, son. I don't know who the fuck this cat is, but I'm ready to set shit off for real," Tone said to his best friend, Kas, as he entered the apartment. Tone took a pull off the blunt he held in his hand as he paced back and forth in Kas' living room.

"Nigga, I tried to tell you, ever since Sugar Foot got knocked, these new motherfuckers been coming in taking over. There's some new shit out they slinging called K2O or some shit like that. It got these fiends going crazy. Niggas can't make a dollar out here. Shit just got real," Kas replied as he blew smoke from his mouth from the cigarette he was smoking.

"Nigga, I need to eat. I'm not letting these niggas stop my flow. I'm about to hit up Rell and see if he knows what this new shit is because I need to re-up real fast. Motherfuckers don't want this shit we slinging. I almost beat the shit out of that nigga Craig crack head ass. Nigga looked at my shit like it was contagious or something. I'm like, 'nigga you're a fucking fiend. You been smoking this same shit for the last few years. Now you looking at my shit like it's not good enough for you.' That shit had me tight," Tone fumed.

"I know, my nigga. That shit happened to me, too, with these fiends over here. I need to see Rell ass, too. You know that nigga don't like talking over the phone. Let's roll to the nigga crib and see what's up," Kas said as he put his cigarette butt in the ashtray.

Kas and Tone headed over to the next building to pay Rell a visit. Kas was five feet eleven inches tall and weighed no more than onne hundred sixty pounds. He was brown skinned and sported a nappy afro. Tone was a caramel complexion standing five feet seven inches tall. He was medium built. The women loved Tone because he was fine with his deep waves and gray eyes. He kept himself looking good for the ladies.

Kas and Tone reached Rell's floor in a matter of seconds, upon entering the building. They didn't waste any time knowing they were thirsty for answers. Tone knocked on the door, once they arrived at Rell's apartment.

"Who is it?" Rell shouted from the other side of the door.

"Nigga, it's Tone," Tone replied. Rell unlocked his door and opened it.

"What's good, niggas? Come in," Rell said. Tone and Kas entered the apartment. "What's going on?" Rell questioned as he closed the door behind them.

"Yo, niggas haven't been able to eat out here. Did you see these new niggas that's been out here slinging some new shit that got these fiends open?" Tone blurted out.

"I heard about it. Yawl niggas need to find out who their supplier is," Rell suggested.

"Nigga, we thought your ass knew where they were getting their shit from. We can't make a dollar out here because these motherfuckers is locking shit down. Those niggas are deep too. I haven't even seen any of Sugar Foot's people out here since that nigga got hit up," Tone explained.

"You niggas need to go and holla at DC. You know that nigga got connections all over and been holding down his side of the woods. Maybe that nigga can shed some light on what's going down over here. I haven't been seeing that many boys around here. When the motherfuckers come around, shit be dead over here. Niggas should be taking advantage of that shit as much as possible. Brownsville always got cops around this mother-fucker but shit hasn't been the same since it quieted down. When niggas get knocked off the map over here, cops are out that day.

but once the body is moved, shit gets quiet. These motherfuckers don't give a fuck about finding the person behind it or nothing. Shit, if you're not the fucking president or a motherfucker in high class, they don't give a fuck about you. This is why I sell my little weed and stay my ass out of sight. I don't have time for shit like this. Motherfuckers we have never seen around here before moves in on other niggas' turfs trying to take over shit. I'm not about to get killed for no block. As long as a motherfucker don't come my way on some bullshit, I'm good," Rell retorted.

"I feel you, my nigga. You got that weed game on lock, though. Everybody knows that your shit is fire. Your hustle isn't going to stop, but me and this nigga Kas' shit is all fucked up. I'm going to see DC ass because I know that motherfucker probably on it already. I'm going to holla at you later Rell," Tone said as he moved toward the door with Kas behind him.

"Yawl niggas stay up," Rell hollered behind them both.

***

Tilden Projects

"Hey, Aunt Sheryl. Hey, what's up, Tadow? I haven't seen you in a minute," Andrea said as she opened the door for her aunt and cousin.

"What's going on, ma? You looking good. How is college life treating you?" Tadow asked as he hugged his cousin.

"It's good. I don't know when I'm going back but I do love school," Andrea replied.

"Hey, Andrea, how is your mom doing?" Sheryl asked.

"She's doing much better, auntie. Go on in the back and see her. Xavier is in their singing to her," Andrea shared as she smiled at the thought of her nephew. He was definitely a smart child.

"What's good, Taz? I didn't even see your ass over there," Tadow said as he walked into the living room and gave Taz B a pound.

"I'm chilling, son. What's up with you? I haven't seen your ass in a minute. What you doing over here?" Taz B questioned.

"I walked my mother over here. Niggas went to her crib looking for me. I had to make sure that she got here safe. Where's Mo?" Tadow asked.

"This is why I told them niggas I was out of this shit. I knew shit like this was going to happen. I'm leaving here as soon as that nigga get his ass back here. I'm not feeling any of this shit. I got too much shit going on in my life to be out here going to war with motherfuckers pushing this shit they got out when I haven't been out there in over seven years. I'm done with that shit and I'm not going back to that lifestyle for nobody," Taz B said. He was serious. Mo had pressed him hard when he was out there selling drugs and pushed him to go to school and get a job. Taz B obliged and this was before their mother had fallen ill. He couldn't understand how Mo could preach to him time and time again about staying off the streets and being a man doing something constructive with his life, and then turn around and ask him to go back to that life style because of their baby brother. Taz B wasn't having it.

"I need to know who the fuck was these niggas that went to my mother's crib looking for me instead of coming to me. That's straight up pussy shit. Luckily, my pops was there and had his uniform on. Otherwise, I would hate to think of what could've happened to my mother. The shit is crazy," Tadow said.

"Mo left here a while ago. He had to go and take care of something, I guess. I don't know when that nigga is coming back. Hit that nigga phone up. I'm sure he will answer, and tell him what happened," Taz B said. He wondered how Mo would feel about knowing that niggas were bringing shit to his aunt now. T Ski was supposed to have the family on watch. Taz B knew that was bullshit. If niggas could easily step to his aunt's crib, they could come to their crib as well.

"I'm about to hit that nigga up right now and let him know that I'm here. I been trying to reach Lee ass. He's probably somewhere laid up with one of his baby mothers. This nigga don't never answer his phone when he's with one of them bitches," Tadow shared.

***

"Look at you. I haven't seen you up out of this bed looking like yourself in so long. How are you feeling, sis?" Sheryl said, smiling at Evelyn. Her sister looked different with all of her hair cut off, but she looked alive and well. That was all that mattered to Sheryl.

"She's still not saying much, auntie, but she's been walking around and laughing. She's using the bathroom on her own," Andrea said proudly.

Evelyn wanted to say something to her sister but she didn't think this was the time. She knew that Sheryl had come to tell her something and she wanted to hear what she had to say before anything.

"Hello, Xavier. You are becoming more handsome every time I see you," Sheryl said to Xavier.

"Thank you, Aunt Sheryl," Xavier said.

"Where's Mo?" Sheryl asked Andrea.

"I don't know. There's so much going on that I don't know what to do, Aunt Sheryl. This environment is not good for mommy, but you know she doesn't want to leave here. I don't know why she still considers to stay out here knowing how dangerous it's becoming," Andrea said.

"Brownsville is not the only dangerous place around, honey. It's not the neighborhood that makes it dangerous, it's the cruel people that's out here that makes it this way. We have been here all of our lives and never had to see the police standing on every corner. There wasn't that much crime going on back then. Now it's just getting out of hand. I was thinking about going to stay with my husband at his mother's house myself. That was the reason I came here to see Evelyn. I wanted to tell her that I wouldn't be here to visit as much once I go to Queens. Some guys came to my house looking for Tadow today, and you know that pissed your uncle off. He's demanding that I leave

Brownsville and go to Queens with him for a while," Sheryl explained. She felt bad that she wouldn't be able to visit her sister as much as she did before, but for the first time, Sheryl was afraid to be alone in her own home after today.

"I understand, auntie, and mommy would understand that as well. She has me here with her and I'm not going anywhere no time soon. I'm going to transfer my transcript and just take my classes online until I know that my mother is okay. Since I been home, she's made so much progress. All she needed was some attention and love. She's going to be okay. I still can't get her to agree on going to see a doctor, but I think she's going to be fine," Andrea said as she smiled at Evelyn. Evelyn smiled back at her daughter.

Sheryl walked over by her sister, who was sitting in the chair that her visitors usually sat in, and kneeled down in front of Evelyn. "Sis, I'm going to come and see you as soon as I get settled in Queens. It might be a few weeks before I can get back over here. I don't want you to think that I have abandoned you. I love you, Ev, and I just need to get away for a while because I don't know what my boys are into in these streets. It's just not safe for me to be home alone right now. But I will be back to see you as much as I can, okay?" Sheryl said with tears falling from her eyes. It was hard to say this to her sister when she was at her bedside every week once Evelyn took ill. She didn't know if it would be her last time speaking to her sister or not because, even though Evelyn looked well, she still had a sickness that could take her out at any given moment.

Evelyn wiped away her sister's tears and pulled her in for a hug. Sheryl hugged her sister tight. Andrea was so moved that she shed a few tears of her own.

"I love you, Ev," Sheryl said.

Chapter 4

Langston Hughes

"What's up, Panama? Is DC around? I need to holla at him real quick," Tone said.

"DC is not here. What's good though?" Panama asked.

"I just wanted to know if the nigga had connects to anyone that was pushing that new shit out. A nigga can't eat in his own hood since niggas started pushing this new shit. Fiends isn't on our shit like that. I can't make a dollar out here to save my damn life," Tone explained.

"Yea, we was told about that shit. DC trying to find out himself who is supplying K2O," Panama said.

"Damn. I guess niggas is going to have to go outside of the hood just to make a fucking buck. This shit is fucking mad, yo. No one has the slightest clue where the shit is coming from and the only motherfuckers that has access to the shit isn't even from around here," Kas explained.

"Yo, my nigga told me that those two niggas, Tadow and Lee, is pushing the shit, too. They have to know who these new cats are that's slinging this shit. I sent some of my peoples to that nigga mom crib to see him but he wasn't there. That nigga pops is a fucking commissioner. That crooked motherfucker might be the one supplying him. Niggas is on it, though, and we will find out what's good. Once we get that shit in our possession, we can give you a good deal on some," Panama said.

"Take my number down. That's a good look," Tone said. Panama took out his phone and typed in Tone's phone number as well as Kas' number. Panama gave them both dap and headed into the building.

Panama was standing outside when Tone and Kas approached him. Niggas had been calling and trying to holla at DC all day. Everyone wanted to know who had K2O. Panama knew that they would make a killing if they could just find the source to get put on to the new drug and sell it to all the local dealers around. Panama headed into the apartment.

"Niggas been coming here left and right asking about that new shit. Once we find out how to get our hands on that shit, we going to make a killing selling that shit to these hungry motherfuckers out here. I just finished talking to Kas and Tone. They were talking about them out of town niggas, too. I think we need to pay these motherfuckers a visit and just take their work from them. These motherfuckers came into the wrong hood trying to push something new and not wanting to plug niggas in," Panama said to DC.

"I'm not moving just yet. If we knock those niggas off right now, we will never get the information to who their suppliers are. We have to map this shit out first. You said these niggas move in packs. These niggas came to a hood that they're not familiar with and started pushing shit out that's taking money out of all the hood hustlers' pockets. They are fearless and they are a strong team. We can't just go at them sideways. I don't want to lose any of my men if they go in unprepared. I'll have this shit figured out by tonight," DC replied.

"Did Cruise find out anything?" Panama asked DC.

"Cruise got his people on it. It's going to be hard finding out where this shit is coming from if we don't at least get to one of them niggas. I hit up all the connections I know as well as a few small timers and no one has heard of this shit. I need to get my hands on the shit and see what the hype is about. I'm trying to figure out how the fuck a new drug comes into the hood in such a short time and has motherfuckers open like that. There's definitely something in that shit to be making these fiends go crazy," DC replied.

"I'm going to see if I can get one of the fiends to cop it for me. I'll bring it back to you in a few," Panama said as he headed toward the door.

DC shook his head. This was becoming a problem and if shit was getting hard for niggas in the other projects, DC knew that his side was going to start losing out as well. DC didn't normally stay in Brooklyn too long. He had a house out in Pennsylvania but would travel back and forth to make sure that his operation was running smoothly out here. DC had just found a spot out in PA where he was about to open up a lounge. He was getting older and needed some insurance. He knew that he could make a killing out there because the town was full of partyers.

Stroudsburg was mostly considered the country part of PA but DC knew that if he opened a lounge out there and could keep it open until at least 4am, being that everything else shut down by 1am, he could bring in a decent income. He had to make sure that money was right out in Brooklyn where all his workers were compensated well, along with his brother, first. DC knew that if he started this war between his people and the out of town niggas, he had to be prepared to lose some of his good men. After speaking with his brother and his best friend, James, DC knew that he had to get a plan together quickly. DC gave his self until tonight to figure out what and how he was going to move.

***

Rikers Island

An hour later, Pablo pulled into a parking space. Mo had decided to tag along with T Ski to see what his next move was. Mo hadn't forgotten what T Ski had mentioned to him earlier, stating he wasn't watching his moves close enough to find out the answers to his questions. Mo definitely needed to know what was going on and was going to watch everything from now on.

Mo looked over at T Ski. T Ski pulled out his cellphone and dialed a number. Mo waited to see what was going to be said over the phone between T Ski in the other person. Mo's phone started to ring as soon as T Ski said "hello" into his phone. Mo looked at his phone and saw that it was Tadow calling. Mo caught an attitude. T Ski had exited the vehicle to talk on the phone in private. Mo pressed the talk button and answered.

"What up?" Mo said.

"Yo, I'm at your crib right now. Where are you?" Tadow questioned.

"What the fuck are you doing at my crib?" Mo said with an attitude.

"My mother came to see your mom. Yo niggas showed up at my mom crib today looking for me and my brother. What the fuck is that all about?" Tadow said, matching Mo's attitude.

"I don't know shit about that. I heard that you and your brother is pushing K2O. You knew that you weren't supposed to get involved with that shit. Why the fuck are you pushing it?" Mo questioned.

"Who said that we couldn't push it? I wasn't told that shit. If that be the case, then why was the shit given to me? You know what the fuck I do. I couldn't care less if niggas come to me with the bullshit, but going to my mother's crib is another fucking story," Tadow replied.

"I'm about to see what's up with that shit. I'm going to hit you back. How long are you going to be at my crib for?" Mo asked, thinking about what Tadow had said. He didn't want anything happening to his aunt and was curious to know who the niggas were that went to her house.

"I don't know. I'm going to be here as long as my mom is here. I'm not letting her walk the streets alone," Tadow replied.

"Shit. Is she good?" Mo asked.

"Yea. My pops was there with her," Tadow said in a calmer tone, being that Mo took his tone down a notch.

"Try to keep her there until I get back home. I'll be there shortly. I'll get to the bottom of this shit," Mo said as he ended the call. Mo was pissed. Tadow was hot and he didn't want him at his crib around his mother, son, and sister, especially now, knowing that niggas came to his mother's crib looking for him. Mo was starting to believe that what Taz B was saying might be true. Mo had to think about his son, mother, and sister. He couldn't take a chance on anything happening to them because of what they were doing.

Mo was mad with Tadow and Lee because they weren't supposed to touch the product. They were supposed to let the niggas that T Ski had put in position push the shit. None of their names were supposed to be attached to K2O. But these dumb ass niggas fucked that up. Mo looked out the window at T Ski, who was no longer on the phone but standing outside the car looking over toward the prison's direction. Mo didn't go into the parking lot and was definitely not getting on the bus to cross the bridge to get to the prison. He didn't know anyone that was on Rikers and didn't think that T Ski knew anyone there either.

Sonovia Alexander

Chapter 5

Riverdale Projects

"What's up, Polo?" Gerry said as he gave his homeboy a pound.

"Same ol' shit, my nigga. Did you hear that niggas shot Lil JB ass, then killed Rob and his girl? Shit is crazy out here. No one seen shit. Streets not talking, and that shit is wild. Niggas usually know something. This shit happened early morning, too," Polo replied.

"Yea, I heard what went down. That's why I came on this side. It's fucking dead over here right now. What's been going down in the hood? I heard a few niggas got hit up," Gerry questioned as he took a cigarette out of his pocket and lit it up.

"Nigga, I don't know. I been hearing shit, too. That's why my black ass go to work and come straight the fuck home. I don't be hanging out here like that. Shit is just too crazy for me. I got seeds to take care of, you feel me? I'm not about to get caught up in no bullshit out here. I'm ready to get my kids up out of here," Polo answered.

"That's what's up. Shit, I haven't been out here since the New Year came in. I got a call from my nigga DC. I was on my way to go check that nigga until I saw your ass sitting out here," Gerry responded.

"Yea, I'm waiting on my girl to get off the bus. I don't trust niggas out here," Polo explained.

"I feel you, son. Yo, who are those niggas standing over there looking suspect?" Gerry questioned looking in the direction where a group of dudes stood posted up in front of the building across from where they stood.

"I don't know. When I came out, they were posted up there. Shit, I don't know any of these new cats that's been showing up over here for the last few days. Niggas said they got some new product out called K2O that got these fiends going crazy over it. I never seen these niggas around here before," Polo replied.

"A'ight, son. Good looking. I'm gon holla at you. Stay up," Gerry said as he gave Polo dap and started walking off. Gerry was sure to get a head count of how many niggas he saw posted up in front of the building. He didn't recognize any of the dudes either. He hadn't been in the hood since the previous year because he had violated his curfew and his parole officer was looking for him. He stayed out of Brownsville, knowing that if he got caught slipping, he was going down.

Gerry pulled out his phone and dialed DC's phone number. He picked up his pace, glancing behind him every few seconds. He didn't know half the niggas around that he had seen so far. There were gangs of niggas posted up in Van Dyke Projects, as well as Brownsville houses. Gerry thought that shit was about to go down the way the niggas were just standing around looking serious.

"What's good, son?" DC said on the other end of the phone.

"Yo, my nigga, you weren't lying. I just passed a few of the projects and it's mad niggas posted around. I didn't recognize any of them either. I just left Riverdale and I just counted at least eight of them niggas posted up. The niggas were just standing around not doing shit. That shit look suspect. I don't see any cops around either. Shit looks real suspect over here," Gerry explained.

"Where you at now?" DC questioned.

"I'm on my way to you right now," Gerry responded.

"If you see that nigga Tadow or his brother Lee, hit them niggas up," DC said.

"I got you, son," Gerry responded. He hung up his phone and placed it back in his pocket. He looked back to make sure no one was following him as he proceeded down the block. Gerry looked around to see if he could locate anyone he knew that might have valuable information for him to report back to DC.

***

Rikers Island

Mo rolled the window down. He had been sitting inside the car for the last twenty minutes. T Ski was busy making calls, and not telling Mo who they were waiting for.

"Yo, I need to talk to you. We need to get back to the house ASAP," Mo said.

"Hold on. He's coming right now," T Ski said.

"Who's coming?" Mo questioned. Mo looked over in the direction where T Ski started walking off to and noticed a guy coming their way.

T Ski met the man and embraced him. Mo couldn't make out who the dude was. He was a distant away but Mo knew that he was soon about to find out. Mo stepped out of the car to get a better look at the man walking side by side with his brother.

Mo couldn't believe who it was once they got close to the vehicle. "Oh shit," Mo said. He smiled as he walked around the car to greet his uncle. He hadn't seen his Uncle Gus in eleven years. He had been arrested along with his father. None of his family ever heard from Gus and assumed that he didn't want any dealings with the family because of the life he lived, or he was dead, one.

"What's up, nephew?" Gus said, hugging his nephew.

"How the fuck you get out? Man, I thought you were dead, real talk. When we used to go visit my pops, you came down once, and after that, we didn't see your ass again. My pops never mentioned you or anything. Damn, it's good to see you," Mo said.

"Yea, I know, young blood. A nigga had to maintain and hold shit down. I couldn't stand the thought of thinking about my family knowing that I was going to be away for so long. A nigga can easily get fucked thinking about the outside instead of what's going on inside those four walls, you feel me?" Gus responded. He couldn't stop smiling. He was finally free after eleven years of prison. He didn't know how he got off and who was responsible for getting him his pardon papers, but he was glad to be out.

"T Ski, we need to get back to the house. Tadow is there with Aunt Sheryl. He told me that some niggas went to Aunt Sheryl's house looking for him and Lee," Mo said to T Ski.

"Mo, go ahead on to the house. I need to drop Uncle Gus off. I'll be right behind you," T Ski said as he started walking off across the street where a black Mercedes truck was parked.

Mo didn't recognize the truck sitting there when they first pulled up. Gus followed T Ski. Mo walked back over to the car and entered the vehicle. He watched as the truck pulled off and passed him by. Mo didn't know who the driver was. Mo shook his head as Pablo started the car and pulled off.

Chapter 6

Tilden Projects

Mo walked into his apartment an hour in a half later. Xavier was in the kitchen eating. When he saw Mo, he smiled and stood from the table to go and greet his father.

"Hi, daddy," Xavier said excitedly.

"What's going on, lil man?" Mo said as he lifted his son up and cradled him in his arms, kissing him on the forehead.

"I'm finishing up my food. Aunt Sheryl made me something to eat while Aunty Andrea taking a bath. I was waiting for you to get back in the house. Are you going back out?" Xavier questioned.

"Not right now. Go ahead and finish up your food. Let me go speak to Tadow real quick," Mo said as he put Xavier down. Mo headed into the living room where Tadow and Taz B were engaged in playing video games.

"Did you find out what's good?" Tadow asked without looking up at Mo.

"Nah. I'll find out though. What have you two niggas been doing with the product?" Mo asked as he sat down in the lazy boy chair trying to keep his voice down.

"We was given two bags and told to give one to a dude named Chris and we kept the other. No one said shit about the other bag. I and Lee pushed that shit ourselves," Tadow said, now putting the remote to the game down and facing Mo.

"You both were told that we were not getting involved in pushing K2O. Why didn't you call me about the other bag? I would have made sure that it was picked up from you guys. Now you got niggas coming to your mother crib looking for you. God knows how many niggas out here is going to be after you two. You both know where the product is coming from because you're pushing the shit yourself. People are going to know who your supplier is. It's only a few niggas that's pushing this shit, and none of them are from Brooklyn. When word gets out, if it hasn't already, that the two of you know about it, they are definitely coming after you," Mo said in almost a whisper.

"I'm not scared of these punk ass niggas out here in the Ville. Nigga, if I get got, then it is what it is. I'm not going down without a fight, though, you can bet your ass that shit. Like I said before, no one told me that we couldn't move this shit. I sold that shit in less than four hours. The fiends couldn't get enough of the shit. They kept coming and sending more fiends over to cop. What the fuck was I supposed to do? Not take the money? Not sell the product? I thought the idea was to get out the word about K2O. It just so happen that Lee and I are known and the word spread just a little bit quicker than planned," Tadow said, trying to maintain his anger.

"Stop being cocky like you hot shit, my nigga. It's not that serious. I'm not your fucking enemy. You did some dumb shit and you know it. If you don't care about your life, that's fine. You need to care about your mother's well-being along with the rest of the women in this family. This is why I shouldn't have put yawl niggas down, because you do what the fuck you want to do anyway," Mo said through clenched teeth.

"I'm a grown ass fucking man. I'm supposed to do what the fuck I want. I been out here doing my thing for the last few years. You haven't been out here holding me down before, and from the way you talking, you won't hold me down now. Why the fuck should it matter to you about what the fuck I do?" Tadow said with an attitude.

"I don't give a fuck about what you do, nigga, until it starts affecting the rest of the family. You were given strict orders and now niggas is after you to get information about the product. What the fuck are you going to do about that, Tadow? You don't give a fuck about shit, right? What about your mother? How the fuck am I or any of us supposed to protect our family if we are doing stupid shit like putting ourselves on blast. You need to clean this shit up. I'm going to find out who it was that went to Aunt Sheryl's house. But keep that shit up and you will be on your own, protecting your own ass," Mo said as he stood from his seat and headed back into the kitchen. He wanted to fuck his cousin up but knew that Xavier was right in the kitchen probably listening to their whole conversation.

"Did you see mommy yet, daddy?" Xavier questioned Mo as soon as he walked into the kitchen.

"Yes. She's awake and she's doing okay," Mo replied as he opened up the refrigerator, grabbing a bottle of water out.

"When can I go and see her?" Xavier asked.

"She said that she's coming to get you tomorrow to take you home with her. Listen, Xavier, I want to talk to you about something real quick," Mo pulled up a chair and sat beside Xavier. "Your mother isn't in her right frame of mind. She was really mad with me today and yelling out all kinds of crazy things like taking you away and me never seeing you again. You know that I will never let that happen, right?" Mo asked his son.

"Yes." Xavier replied.

"When you see your mother tomorrow, don't mention what I said to you. If she tries to leave town with you, you make sure you get to a phone and call me," Mo said.

"I will, daddy," Xavier responded.

"That's my boy. When you're done eating, we can go in the back and do something together. You still like playing checkers, right?" Mo inquired. He didn't really know exactly what his son was interested in. It upset him but he was going to fix that soon enough.

"Yes. I don't think you're going to beat me so maybe we should play my video games."

Mo laughed at his son. He thought that was cute and knew that Xavier was probably right.

"I will definitely give you some competition with the video games. Finish up your food, then meet me in the room. I'm going to check up on your grandma," Mo said as he headed out of the kitchen toward his mother's room.

***

Plaza Projects

"Yo, get DC on the phone real quick. There go that nigga Lee right there walking with his baby moms," Cali said to Drew. They were two of DC's workers.

"I'm hitting him up now. Yo, don't lose that nigga. I don't want him to get away. This nigga slipping and walking around like he's tough and shit. We definitely gotta get that nigga," Drew explained. "Yo, DC, I'm out here in the Plaza and I just spotted the nigga Lee. He's walking around with his baby moms. Do you want us to get at this nigga?" Drew asked.

"Blast that motherfucker. Let me know once you get his ass. I know Tadow will be heading over there soon after, then we will get that nigga. This shit is going better than I planned. See if that nigga will talk, and if not, get his ass. Hit me back when it's done," DC said as he disconnected the call.

"Let's go," Drew ordered. Drew pulled his pistol out of the back of his pants and held it in his hand. Cali was right beside him with his nine drawn. They crossed the street and couldn't believe how easy this was going to be. Lee was so busy arguing with his baby's mom that he didn't see Cali or Drew run up on him. Drew opened fire, along with Cali.

Boom. Boom. Boom. Boom. A total of four bullets ripped through Lee's body, dropping him to the ground.

"Who's your supplier, nigga?" Drew asked.

Lee picked up his hand and flipped him the finger. Drew smiled wickedly before putting a bullet in Lee's head. Karen started screaming. Drew looked up at Karen and pointed the gun at her and let off one shot into her head. She dropped dead beside Lee. Drew and Cali ran off, heading toward Glenmore Projects.

Drew grabbed his phone out of his pocket as he slowed his pace to dial DC's number. DC picked up on the first ring. "It's done. Nigga wouldn't talk," Drew said and hung up the phone, picking up his speed to catch up to Cali.

Sonovia Alexander

Chapter 7

Newport Gardens

Josiah heard a tap at the door. He walked over with his gun in hand to see who was knocking so lightly. Josiah looked through the peephole and had to stare for a minute at the face that was opposite the door.

"Who is it?" Rabbit asked grabbing his gun ready to start blasting. Josiah had paused for a second too long for Rabbit.

"You're not going to believe who is on the other side of the fucking door, my nigga," Josiah said, tucking his gun in the front of his pants. He opened the door and stood face to face with his brother Gus.

"I'm home, motherfuckers," Gus said, smiling hard.

Josiah embraced his brother. He was glad to see him. Everyone thought that he and Po were going to spend their last days in prison. There would be no life left for them to live once they were due to be released.

"How the fuck you get out, man?" Josiah asked as he closed the door behind him.

Gus hugged Rabbit as well. They were all excited to see each other. This was a reunion that they would never forget.

"Man, I can't tell you that because I don't know the answer myself. I know that they sent for me yesterday and brought me from upstate here to Rikers, and I was released today. T Ski brought me over here. Hell, it was him and Mo that picked me up from Rikers. That young motherfucker got some brains on him. That nigga was telling me some shit. I couldn't wait to get up in here to find out what nephew was talking about," Gus said as he sat his small duffle bag down on the floor.

"Yo, nephew is the truth. I don't know much but one of our people sent for us. Po called us and told me to follow his instructions. I had to clap a few niggas but shit is live out here, bro. Shit, I'm not even sure who we are working for, but I know the money is good and it's family," Josiah explained.

"Damn, you don't know who the fuck in our family is getting it like that?" Gus asked.

"I can't call it, bro. Fuck all that, how does it feel to be home, nigga? Big black ass nigga. You all swelled the fuck up like you been taking steroids for breakfast, lunch, and dinner," Josiah joked.

"Shut the fuck up, nigga. Ain't shit to do in prison but work out. Man, I thought this day would never come. Yawl know a nigga can't wait to get some real food and shit. I need to eat," Gus said.

"Oh we definitely going to feed you, bro, then we heading over to a strip joint to get you right for your home coming. Shit, I wish I knew ahead of time you was getting out, I would've planned something for you," Rabbit said.

"Fuck that. You still can do something for me. I haven't had pussy in eleven years. A nigga gon' fuck around and catch a fucking heart attack trying to bust that first nut," Gus joked. The brothers erupted in laughter.

"You don't want to hit up your wife? I'm sure Denise ass will be ready for your ass," Josiah said.

"She doesn't know I'm home. I'm not going to pop up on her ass either, not knowing if she got a nigga up in her crib. I'm just coming home and not ready to go back to the joint for putting a nigga to sleep," Gus explained.

"I feel you. I check on her all the time and she spends most of her time at the nursing home working or home with your grandkids. I don't see niggas in and out of there so you better try to get back in good and save your marriage. Shit, she didn't divorce your ass after all of the years you been away. That should mean something," Rabbit explained.

"Yea, I'll hit her up after yawl show me a night of fun. I'm not about to get my hopes up and be disappointed. A nigga need to at least smell some pussy before being denied his old pussy, you feel me?" Gus mentioned. The brothers laughed again. "I thought my ass was going to have to fuck one of them young niggas up downstairs. They were looking at me crazy, but they didn't say shit though. I'm telling you I would've snapped one of them niggas' neck," Gus remarked.

"Nah, those are niggas pushing out this new shit that one of our people got out called K2O. That shit got these fucking crack heads out here bugging over that shit. They are a tight team and they taking over shit out here in the Ville. You will see for yourself in a few how live shit is out here," Josiah said.

"Well which one of our people are you talking about? I have never heard of no shit like that before," Gus replied.

"Shit, I don't know who got that shit popping like that, but it's some new shit. They selling the shit thirty dollars a pop," Josiah explained.

"Damn, and these fiends could afford that shit?" Gus said seriously.

Josiah and Rabbit chuckled. They thought the same shit at first. They were the ones supplying the men with the product.

They saw how quick these cats were coming back to re-up. Word spread real fast amongst crack heads.

"Shit is definitely crazy out here, boy. You missed a lot of shit. Things have changed since you were last out here on these mean streets of Brooklyn," Josiah confessed.

"Wait a minute, if you and Po got locked up for damn near the same shit, why isn't he home?" Rabbit questioned.

"Man, didn't I tell you I don't know what the fuck is going on. I'm still unsure of how my black ass got out. Whoever got me off, I will be eternally grateful to them. Po and I wasn't in the same facility, so it wasn't like I could reach out to him to ask him what was going on," Gus replied.

"The whole set up and how shit is going is like a fucking puzzle. Niggas don't know who the fuck is behind the operation. All I know is that they are calling shots and making shit happen. The nigga know when the police are coming, nigga directs you on how to move and act after a stint as if he's right there beside us watching the whole thing unfold. The shit is sick but, as long as I'm getting what's due to me, I'm good," Rabbit explained.

"I feel you. I'm trying to stay the fuck out of jail. I never thought I would get my freedom and get to walk out of prison alive. I need to know that whatever it is niggas got going on, that shit don't send me back in. I will die before going back to jail and I mean that shit," Gus remarked.

"I feel you, bro. Let's go get you something to eat. We can talk about that shit later on. Nigga, you home now. It's time to get you out to have a little fun," Josiah said.

Chapter 8

Tilden Projects

"Aunt Sheryl and Tadow left already?" Andrea asked, walking into the kitchen where Mo sat with Xavier.

"I know you weren't in the bathroom that long?" Mo said over his shoulder.

"I was relaxing and it felt good to unwind in a nice hot bubble bath. Where's Taz B and T-Ski at?" Andrea questioned as she stretched her arms.

"Taz is in the living room asleep and T-Ski didn't get in yet. Do you remember Uncle Gus?" Mo asked Andrea.

"Of course I remember Uncle Gus crazy ass. What about him?" Andrea hadn't heard anything about her uncles from her father's side since her dad went to jail.

"He came home today," Mo said.

"For real? That's good. I hope he stay out of trouble. Does Aunt Denise know he's home? I'm sure his kids and grandkids are going to be happy to see him," Andrea said in a low tone, wishing that it was her father reuniting with his family.

"I'm not sure. T Ski took him somewhere and I came straight home," Mo explained.

Mo's phone started going off just as T Ski was unlocking the door to the house. Mo looked at his caller ID and noticed it was Tadow calling. Mo answered just to make sure that he and his aunt had made it back to her house safely.

"Yo," Mo said into the phone.

"Mo. Mo," Tadow said through sobs. Mo stood up knowing that something was wrong.

"What happened?" Mo asked aloud.

"Lee dead. They killed him. Him and his baby moms. My brother body is lying out here on the hard cold streets while these motherfuckers are walking around with their life. I'm killing every fucking body, I swear," Tadow screamed into the phone with tears falling from his eyes.

"What the fuck? Oh shit. Where you at? I'm on my way," Mo shouted.

T Ski and Taz B were both ready to roll out with their brother, knowing that something serious had just gone down.

"I'm at my crib right now. One of his baby mom friends called my mother and told her what happened. My pops is out there with my mom. I can't see my brother like that, man. They still got his body out there uncovered. They shot him down like he was a stray dog. What the fuck am I going to do without my brother?" Tadow screamed. He was truly hurting behind losing his brother. That was his ride or die and his best friend. He loved Lee more than he loved his own life. Tadow tried to reach him but couldn't. He knew that whoever it was that had paid his mother a visit earlier on that day was the one behind his brother's death.

"Don't go anywhere, Tadow. I'm on my way," Mo said as he hung up the phone. He wiped his own tears from his eyes. Although he was mad at his cousin earlier on that day, that didn't stop him from loving him. Mo's heart ached at this moment to find out that one of his own relatives was gunned down in the streets.

"What happened?" Andrea screamed. She was already crying even though she didn't know what was going on. She saw the tears fall from Mo's eyes and knew that most likely someone had died. Andrea thought that it was probably their grandmother since she was old, but the voice on the other end of the phone made the call seem like something had gone down in the streets.

"Lee is dead," Mo confessed. He looked at T Ski who looked like he had transformed into the devil. Mo had witnessed T Ski getting angry a few days ago, but the look that he had on his face at this moment made Mo nervous. "T-Ski, you good, bro?" Mo asked his brother.

"Nah. Stay in the house," T Ski ordered.

Mo looked at his brother like he was crazy. "Bro, I can't do that. I have to go check on Tadow and Aunt Sheryl," Mo explained.

"No. I got this. Stay here," T Ski said.

"You said you had this shit before but now our cousin is dead. Is this a part of your plan, T Ski?" Taz B asked. He knew that someone was going to get killed behind this madness.

"Shut the fuck up, pussy. I didn't say shit to you. It should've been you that caught that bullet instead of Lee," T Ski said before walking out of the apartment and slamming the door behind him.

Mo, Andrea, and Taz B all stood there in total shock at what T Ski had just confessed to his own brother.

"Oh my God. I don't believe he just said that to his own brother. Mo, T Ski is losing his fucking mind," Andrea said with fresh tears falling from her eyes.

"Andrea, take Xavier in the room," Mo had forgotten that his son was sitting in the kitchen and had heard everything.

Evelyn heard everything and made her way out of her bedroom into the kitchen where her children were. Taz B saw her shadow out of the corner of his eyes, being that he was in the hallway between the kitchen and the bedroom.

"Ma, what are you doing out of your room?" Taz B asked as he ran over to his mother. Mo and Andrea both headed out of the kitchen to go check on Evelyn.

"Mama, what are you doing out of bed?" Andrea shouted.

"I need to go and be with my sister," Evelyn said in a little above a whisper.

Mo and Taz B both looked at each other, shocked at how their mother was walking and speaking like there wasn't anything wrong with her.

"T Ski wants us to stay in the house, ma. Let's get you back in the room in bed," Andrea said, grabbing her mother gently by her arm, trying to guide her back to her bedroom.

"Andrea, let me go. I'm going to be with my sister. T Ski isn't my father, and don't tell me what to do. I'm going out," Evelyn said.

Evelyn was fully dressed in white pants, a white shirt, and her white sneakers. She was going out no matter what her kids said. She knew that Sheryl had been there for her and she had to be there now for her sister. For the last few days, she could feel her strength coming back. She would wait until Andrea was asleep to crawl out of bed and walk over to the window. She would say a prayer in hopes that God would get her out of the funk she was in. The contents that T Ski would give her twice a day also played a big part in her feeling well. She didn't know what it was that her son was giving her, but she was glad that he did. She hadn't felt like herself in months.

Mo went into his room that was past his mother's to go retrieve his gun. Mo went into his closet and grabbed his gun out of the shoe box that was at the top in the far corner and placed his pistol in the small of his back. He had to make sure that he did everything in his power to protect his mother since she insisted on going to be with her sister.

Mo walked back into the hallway and saw that his mother was already at the door. Andrea had put a jacket over her mother, being that it was cool outside.

"Andrea, you and Taz stay here and keep the doors locked. Keep an eye on Xavier. I'll be back as soon as I can," Mo said. He grabbed his phone and dialed T Ski's number. The phone rang out. T Ski didn't answer.

Mo sent him a text message telling T Ski that their mother was out of bed and insisting on going to Aunt Sheryl's house to be there for her. He couldn't stop her and they were heading there now. Mo went to put his phone away when the phone beeped, letting him know that he received a message. He clicked the message open and saw that T-Ski responded, *It's fine.* Mo shook his head and walked side by side with his mother toward the elevator.

"I don't need you to watch over me. I'm fine, Mo," Evelyn said.

Her words weren't as clear as she wanted them to be, but Mo was glad that she was out of bed and speaking. He hoped that this tragedy would help his mother appreciate life more and live hers to the fullest. Mo still wanted to know if his mother was doing this to keep him from living his own life or if she really was in a stupor.

"Ma, what the hell is going on? One minute I'm thinking you're on your death bed and the next you're walking around talking like nothing was ever wrong with you. All these months I couldn't get you to say a word. All you did was stay closed in your room. Did it take something like this to happen for you to get up out of your bed and walk and talk?" Mo asked.

"I'm sick, Mo. But I'm not dead yet. I shut down because I wanted to. That didn't mean that I didn't know how to talk, I just chose not to. I was in a deep depression. This disease took over my mind and my will to live. But I had no choice but to get up and go be with the one that has been here for me since day one," Evelyn explained in a soft tone.

"I have been here since day one. Ma, my girl almost died because I wasn't there to protect her. She won't have nothing to do with me. She blamed me for neglecting her and Xavier because I been here looking after you," Mo said with his eyes tearing up. He was already messed up behind the death of Lee, but now he was feeling all his emotions consume him at once.

"Did I ask you to come and be with me? You did it because you wanted to. I had fallen into a stupor. I didn't know when my last day here on earth was going to be. I will not apologize for you being here to look after me when I gave your life. I didn't ask for you to put your life on hold. I would've died here peacefully and would've still loved you the same, even if you weren't here. It was you, your brothers, your sister, and my grandson that gave me a purpose for wanting to live. I'm sorry about Bella and hope that things will work out for the both of you, but don't blame me," Evelyn said as she pressed the button for the elevator.

Mo was about to respond until he heard the door open from the staircase. Mo grabbed his gun and pointed it in the direction. He was ready to fire until he saw his father standing there.

"Oh my God," Mo said. Mo turned and looked at his mother and moved aside so she could see who was home.

"Po?" Evelyn mumbled. She couldn't believe that her husband was standing in the hallway.

"Hey, baby. Did you miss me?" Po said with a wide grin plastered across his face.

Evelyn walked over to meet her husband and fell into his arms. She cried like a baby. Po held on to his wife for dear life. Mo wiped his tears from his face. This was definitely becoming one of the most emotional days of his life. Mo placed his gun back into the small of his back. He started walking toward the apartment. Po moved in the direction of the apartment, not letting Evelyn go.

"No. I have to go and be with Sheryl," Evelyn said as she pulled back from Po.

"Sheryl is going to be fine. I just left her. You can call her on the phone, but you're not going out there," Po said as he grabbed Evelyn by the hand and led her to the apartment. She didn't object.

Mo opened the door wide and held it open for his parents to enter. Taz B and Andrea both stood in shock at the sight of their father.

"Dad," Andrea shouted. She ran over to her father and hugged him. They were all emotional at this point. Andrea had just wished that she would have this kind of reunion with her own father and here he was in the flesh, standing before her, looking the same as he did ten years ago.

"I missed you all so much," Po said, kissing his daughter on her forehead. He reached over and gave Taz-B a pound and a hug. Po led Evelyn into the living room to get her off her feet.

Mo was so excited that he needed to call someone. He dialed Bella's number without even thinking about what had transpired between the two of them earlier.

Bella answered her phone. "I thought I told you not to call me or ever see me again. What do you want, Mo?" Bella asked angrily.

"Bella, I need someone to talk to. My cousin has just been shot dead and now my father just been released from prison. My emotions are all over the fucking place right now," Mo said.

"Congratulations and sorry for your loss. Is that all?" Bella snapped.

"What did I do so wrong to you for you to be acting this way? I know we argued before the day someone broke into your apartment, but it wasn't me that did it," Mo asked.

"It might as well have been you," Bella stated.

"Why would you say that?" Mo said angrily as he headed to his room so his family wouldn't overhear his conversation.

"It was T Ski that tried to kill me," Bella said as she ended the call.

Mo's mouth dropped wide open. Mo hadn't reached his room yet when he stopped and leaned up against the wall after hearing the news from Bella. Mo felt like someone had just knocked the wind out of him. He knew that something couldn't be right. T Ski would never harm someone that he loved. Bella had to be lying or on some heavy drugs. Mo couldn't think clearly. This was just too much for him to endure in such a short time. He didn't know if he should be sad that he had just lost a loved one or happy that his father was out of prison. His emotions were all over the place.

"Daddy, are you okay? You don't look too well," Xavier said as he stood in front of Mo.

Mo looked at his son and opened his mouth to say something but words didn't come. Mo slid down the wall and sat down on the floor. He had to think about what Bella had just said to him.

Mo thought back to the day T Ski came to the apartment when he had phoned him explaining what had just happened to Bella. It was T Ski that had gone to the back and did something to help get Bella's breathing back.

Mo thought about the visit to the hospital earlier and how Bella's attitude changed once T Ski had passed her room. Bella had to see him. Mo could feel his blood rising. If T Ski had anything to do with Bella getting hurt, he was going to hurt his brother. Although, Mo was a firm believer in blood being thicker than water, he couldn't let this ride.

Xavier sat beside his father and leaned his head on Mo's shoulder. "It's going to be okay, daddy. I know you're sad because your cousin expired. I'm sad too," Xavier said.

Mo looked down at his son and wrapped his arm around him. Mo held on to him as he let the tears fall from his eyes. He felt like he was having a break down. Mo tried to pull himself together, not wanting his son to see him like this, but he couldn't. The more he thought about Bella, and Lee, the more the tears came.

Chapter 9

Po stood from his seat in the living room and was heading toward the kitchen to get himself something to drink when he noticed Mo and a young boy sitting in the hallway. Po approached Mo and stared down at who he knew had to be Mo's son.

"Hello. I'm your grandpa Po. How you doing little man?" Po said to Xavier.

Xavier looked up and smiled at his grandpa. T Ski had told him all about his grandfather and showed him pictures. He was happy to see him for the first time.

"Hi, grandpa. I'm okay. I'm glad your home," Xavier replied.

Po smiled at his grandson. "Thank you. Why don't you go in the living room with grandma and your aunty and let me talk to your dad for a minute?" Po said.

"Okay." Xavier removed Mo's arms from around him and stood to do as he was told. Po slid down the wall, sitting beside Mo.

"When did you get out?" Mo managed to say as he wiped the tears away from his eyes.

"I got out today. Some guy name Pablo was there to pick me up. I know you fucked up behind losing your cousin, son, and

I'm sorry to hear about that. What's been going on since I been away?" Po asked.

"It's too much to even get into right now." Mo had mixed emotions. He loved his brother dearly but he wasn't too happy about what Bella was accusing him of. Mo was told that the hit was supposed to be from Barry's people. Mo didn't know what to believe at this point. He knew that he needed to speak with T Ski and get the answers he wanted.

"I'm going to stay in here with your mother and see about her. Why don't you go on over there and check on your cousin? I will be right here when you get back so we can talk," Po remarked.

Mo wiped his face with the bottom of his shirt as he leaned his right arm against the wall to help him up from the floor. Po stood as well.

"It's good to have you home, pop," Mo said as he hugged his father. For a second, he felt like a kid again, embracing his father. It was a loving hug that he had truly missed.

Mo checked his back, feeling for his gun. It was still intact. Mo started off toward the door. He didn't go to the living room to check on his son or mother. He was desperate now more than ever to find out what the hell was going on with T Ski.

***

Mo reached outside of the building and ran into Ron D. He was just the man Mo was looking for.

"Did you see my brother out here?" Mo asked Ron D.

"I saw him a little while ago get inside of a black suburban. I can't tell you where he's at now," Ron D said.

"This shit is crazy. I'm about to go check on my cousin to make sure that he's good. That nigga taking this shit hard," Mo explained.

"I know the feeling, man. Those two were real close. I'm sorry about Lee. That was my nigga, for real. Let me walk with you over there. I'm not doing shit right now," Ron D offered.

Mo was about to object but thought against it. He knew that someone could easily try to catch him slipping and get at him. He felt better knowing that he had one of his ride or dies by his side. Mo hated the idea of having to watch his back.

"Good looking, son," Mo said as he started off heading to check on his family.

"The coroners is out there now. Hopefully, they picked his body up off the damn streets. I had walked over in that direction once I heard who it was but it was flooded with cops and they weren't letting no one by. The only niggas crazy enough to fuck with your blood is DC boys. No one else is moving like that since their people has been knocked off," Mo looked at Ron D with a raised brow.

"Why the fuck would DC want to kill my family? Niggas didn't fuck with his turf," Mo stated.

"Niggas knew that they had to get to one of them because they out here slinging that new shit that's out here. You already know once niggas found out that someone they knew from the hood was affiliated with the connections, they were going after them," Ron D explained.

"A dead man can't talk. What was the point of killing him if they wanted to know who their supplier is? That shit don't make any sense to me," Mo replied.

"Think about it, Mo. If they kill those two, that's two niggas that won't be pushing weight for them. I'm sure that nigga got his goons waiting to get a taste of that new shit. You know how the game goes, my nigga," Ron D remarked.

Mo walked in silence. He had to let all this new information sink in. He was pissed at his cousins for pushing that shit and this was the main reason why. Mo didn't think that his family would die over it though. That was another reason why he was mad as hell. T Ski said that he kept watch over the family at all times. How the hell didn't he see that coming, or did he see it coming but did nothing to stop it from happening? Mo took his phone out of his pocket and dialed T Ski's number. Mo stopped walking when he heard the operator come on the line saying that the number Mo had called had been temporarily disconnected.

"You good, my nigga?" Ron D said.

"Yea," Mo continued to walk, wondering had he dialed the wrong number. Mo dialed the number again and got the same recording. Mo shook his head in disbelief. He knew that shit wasn't right. He was going to deal with this after making sure that his family was good.

***

"How are you feeling, baby?" Po asked Evelyn.

She lifted her head up off his shoulder to stare him in the eyes. She still couldn't believe that he was home. She didn't want to know how he got out. She was just glad to have her husband home with her, even if it was only for a short while.

"I'm feeling a lot better. I have been taking this medicine that has been giving me all of my strength back. I'm just taking it day by day, you know," Evelyn said.

"I thought you haven't been to the doctor in a long time. How are you taking meds?" Po asked curiously.

"T Ski has been giving me something to take over the last few weeks. I don't know what it is to be exact, but it's working," Evelyn said with half a smile.

"I'm glad to hear that it's working. What exactly is going on with T Ski?" Po inquired.

"I can't really tell you because I'm not sure," Evelyn replied.

Po took a good look at his wife before responding. "Why did you cut your hair off?" Po didn't realize it until now that his wife no longer had her dreads. She was still beautiful and actually looked years younger.

"It was falling out. Andrea cut it for me and we're going to start it from scratch. It will be healthier now," Evelyn replied.

"You're still beautiful, baby. I missed you so much. It feels so good to be back home," Po said as he stretched his legs out.

"Pop, did you know that your brother Gus came home today?"

Po looked at his daughter.

"What do you mean Gus is home? How is that possible?" Po knew after he spoke those words that it could be possible, being that he was home.

"That's what Mo told us today. He and T Ski picked him up today," Andrea added.

"Where is he now?" Po asked.

"I'm not sure. You're going to have to ask Mo."

"I will definitely ask him when he gets back here. Give me a phone as a matter of fact. I have to hear this shit for myself to make sure that it's true," Po said. This was turning out to be a good day for him in spite of what his wife and kids were going through.

Andrea passed Po her cell phone. Po quickly punched in Josiah's number. He put the phone to his ear and waited for his brother to answer.

"Who dis?" Josiah asked.

"This is your fucking brother, nigga," Po said with excitement in his voice and a wide smile across his face.

"Po, oh hell no. Tell me your ass is home too, my nigga," Josiah stated cheerfully.

"I'm at my crib right now with my family. I'm home, baby. I just got word that Gus touched Brooklyn too," Po recited.

"That nigga right here with us. Yo, what the fuck did yawl niggas do? Did yawl pay off someone on the inside to get the both of you crazy niggas out?" Josiah joked.

"Nigga, if I had that kind of money or pull, I would've been home years ago. I need to get up with you fools. Come by my crib when yawl get the chance. I'm dealing with a situation with my wife. Lee got bodied a lil while ago," Po explained.

"We was just with this nigga. What the fuck happened?" Josiah asked.

"I'll holla at you when you reach here. Let me get off this phone." Po ended the call. He saw the look in Evelyn's eyes when he mentioned what happened to Lee. He knew how his wife felt about her family, but he wasn't letting her out of his sight for one minute. He didn't know what kind of effect it would have on her if she saw her nephew's body lying on the streets with parts of his brain splattered across the pavement. He knew that Evelyn wasn't well from what T Ski had told him and he wasn't about to lose her.

Po pulled Evelyn close to him and held her in his arms.

Chapter 10

Riverdale Projects

Mo reached his cousin's apartment. He turned the knob and entered the unlocked door. Ron D was right behind Mo as they both walked toward the back of the apartment since the kitchen and living room were empty. Mo knocked on Tadow's bedroom door. He knew that he was inside because he could hear his sobs on the opposite side of the door. Mo opened the door and stopped before he could move. Mo's heart felt like it fell from his body when he saw Tadow holding a .45 to his head while soaking in his tears.

"Tadow, cuz, please don't do it. Put the gun down. You know this will kill your mother if she lose both her boys. Come on, put the gun down, please," Mo pleaded.

Tadow didn't hear anything Mo said. He was in his own little world. He continued to cry as he thought about his brother's lifeless body laying out on the streets.

Mo walked toward Tadow slowly, hoping that he wouldn't pull the trigger. "Tadow, you don't want to do this," Mo said as he inched closer to his cousin. He tried to contain his own tears from falling. He knew that now was not the time for him to break down. He had to save his cousin from himself.

"Why Lee? Why you? Why not me?" Tadow said.

Mo's heart ached for his cousin. He never wanted to be put in this position of losing someone he loved who was his own flesh and blood.

Mo slowly reached for the gun, hoping that Tadow wouldn't do anything stupid. Mo was a bit nervous because Tadow had his finger wrapped around the trigger. He knew that he had to move with caution.

"I'm going to kill all those niggas for what they did to you, bro. I can't let them get away with it," Tadow spat. Tadow removed his finger off the trigger and Mo snatched the gun out of his hand. "What the fuck are you doing?" Tadow said as he looked up at Mo. He didn't know how or when Mo had come into his apartment.

"Calm down, cuz. I been here for a few minutes. You left your door unlocked. I didn't want you to hurt yourself," Mo spoke in a soft tone.

"I can't believe these motherfuckers killed my brother. Where the fuck was our protection, Mo? You said that we were all being protected. Was that bullshit?" Tadow spat with anger arising in his voice.

"Calm down, Tadow. I don't know what the hell happened. I never wanted anything to happen to any of us. We will get the niggas responsible for this, I promise you that," Mo remarked.

"That ain't gon' bring my brother back. This shit is killing me. I would've given my life for that nigga to keep his. I told that nigga to always keep his fucking phone on. They killed the nigga baby moms. What the fuck is going to happen to his seeds. They don't have a mother or father. This shit is all fucked up," Tadow's legs started shaking beyond his control. He was hot and ready to take anyone's life at this point. He didn't have nothing to lose. He would love to join his brother on the other side.

"I know, cuz. I'm fucked up behind this shit. Some crazy shit is going down and I don't know what the fuck to make of it. My Uncle Gus and my father is home," Tadow looked at Mo with a questioning glare.

"How the fuck those two niggas get out when they were facing twenty-five years to life?" Tadow was confused. It took his mind off his brother for a brief moment so he could collect himself. He didn't notice Ron D standing off by his door.

"I was on my way to bring my mother here to check on you and Aunt Sheryl until my pops came running up the stairs, catching up to us before we could get on the elevator," Mo explained. He could see the change in Tadow's mindset. He felt a little more at ease knowing that he could talk about something else other than Lee.

"Wait a minute, how the fuck was Aunt Evelyn coming to check up on my mom if she has been confined to her bed for months. Nigga, are you playing games with me?" Tadow asked.

"Nigga, does it look like I'm playing. My mom has been getting her strength back and Andrea has been helping her walk and try to do things on her own," Mo replied.

"I'm glad that she's doing much better. That's a blessing. At least I could hear some good news. My bad, Ron D. What's good, homie?" Tadow stood from his bed and walked over toward Ron D to shake his hand.

"I'm good, son. Sorry for your loss," Ron D shared.

"Man, this shit got me fucked up. I loved the shit out of that nigga. You know I won't be able to rest until I find out who the fuck is responsible for this shit," Tadow retorted.

"I got word that DC boys got something to do with that. Niggas was after the both of you because they want that connect," Ron D shared.

"How the fuck did those niggas think that they were going to get our connections if they killed us. Fucking dummies," Tadow took his gun from out of Mo's hand and placed it in the small of his back.

"That was the same shit I asked. Niggas doing shit ass backwards. Where's your mom?" Mo questioned.

"She's back at her crib. We can head over there in a second. Let me wash my face before I head out in the streets. I'm telling you now, if I run into anyone down with that nigga, I'm taking them out."

Mo didn't respond. He felt the same way.

Mo and Ron D walked back toward the door to wait on Tadow. Mo pulled out his phone again and tried reaching T Ski but wound up with the same results. Mo was fuming. He didn't want to make a scene so he put his phone back in his pocket and focused on the matter at hand.

***

Downtown Brooklyn

"Why are we meeting here when you know that my son was just killed? I need to be with my wife. Do you know what I had to go through just to get her to let me leave the house?" Perry explained.

"I understand that, but we have bigger fish to fry. I wired all the money and my pops and uncle are out now. I invented the newest and high profile technology for the police headquarters. Our deal is done. I will still be at the meeting tomorrow, but right now I can't be in Brooklyn. I need for you to try and get the streets cleared up before midnight because it's about to be a lot going down tonight. Mo and Tadow aren't going to rest until they know who's behind the murder of Lee. That has to be handled tonight. You need to get Tadow out of Brooklyn. Don't take no for an answer. He's dealing with too many emotions right now," T Ski explained.

"I thought my sons were protected. You told me that they wouldn't get hurt. How did this happen if you're supposed to be watching over them?" Perry questioned, trying to contain his tears.

"Lee and Tadow was moving product and they weren't supposed to. It was going to happen one way or another. One, if not both, of them were going to get caught up because they were playing by their own rules. They were told to be easy and stick to what they were told to do. I have men all around doing what they have to do. I won't be looking out for anyone that doesn't want to take orders. You know how things work out here. I love my family to death but I can't save them if they want to do their own thing. Give this address to Mo and have him meet me there by 10pm. Tell him to come alone. I'll be by to see my aunt tomorrow evening," T Ski said. He walked off without waiting for a response from his uncle.

Perry stood there looking at his nephew. He couldn't believe that a once quiet and sweet kid could turn out to be so heartless and cruel. Perry was in too deep to get out without getting caught up in the whole operation. He regretted having partaken in T Ski's plan now.

T Ski entered the vehicle that was double parked in the street waiting on him. T Ski's heart hurt for his cousin. He didn't want Lee to die, but he knew that he had to let niggas in the street think that they held weight. Little did they know, T Ski knew who they were and where they lived. T Ski pulled out his laptop and opened up the screen. He looked on and watched as the scene unfolded with his cousin. He was glad that his body was moved from the scene. T Ski shook his head, knowing that it broke his aunt's heart losing a child. He could've saved Lee but it was an eye opener for all of them, T Ski thought. It was going to be a long while before the scene would be cleared up. He could see more police arriving along with crime scene investigators. T Ski shook his head.

Chapter 11

Bedford Stuyvesant
Malcolm X Blvd

Mo arrived at the location his uncle had given him. He couldn't wait to see his brother. Mo was still mad at his brother and hoped that he had a logical reason why he tried to hurt his girl. Mo knocked on the door and waited for someone to answer. He had spoken briefly with his pops and made sure that his son was good before leaving the apartment. Mo had taken a shower and redressed in some dark jeans and a white t-shirt. He let his dreads hang loose. Mo felt more relaxed that his aunt was safe and that his uncle had taken her out of Brooklyn. Perry had even convinced Tadow to go out to Queens with him and Sheryl.

A young Spanish dude answered the door a minute later. He already knew who Mo was. He opened the door wide enough for Mo to enter. Mo stepped inside of the apartment and wondered where T Ski was.

"You can go into the back," the young guy said. Mo looked the young boy over. He didn't look a day over fifteen. He was dressed in all black. He had a short curly fro and a baby face.

Mo proceeded down the hallway leading to the first door he saw on the right. He stopped in front of the door and was amazed by the sight in front of him. There was a big machine standing in the middle of the floor and it made a noise like a washing machine. Mo wasn't sure what the machine was used for and didn't ask. There were scales and chemicals all around the room, and two men seated mixing up something.

"It's the next room," the young guy stated, walking up behind Mo.

Mo looked back over his shoulder as he moved toward the next room. Mo then spotted T Ski sitting behind a computer. There were four desks in the large room with computers on top of each one. There were two other guys in the room with T Ski.

"T Ski," Mo called out to get his brother's attention. T Ski looked up and saw Mo standing there. T Ski typed in a few things on the computer and stood from his seat. He walked over in the direction of Mo.

"Come with me," T Ski said as he bypassed Mo and walked across the room into another. This room had two sets of bunk beds inside. T Ski waited until Mo was inside the room before closing the door behind him.

"T Ski, what the fuck is going on? Tadow is going crazy behind Lee's death. You changed your fucking number on me and I couldn't get ahold to you. Pops is out of jail and I don't know how or when that happened. On top of all of that, I spoke to Bella and she told me you were the one that tried to kill her. Please tell me that isn't true," Mo said in one breath.

T Ski stood there for a brief moment without blinking an eye. He knew that he had to choose his words wisely when talking to Mo. His brother was vulnerable and going through a lot. T Ski didn't want to push him to his limit and make Mo snap.

"Mo, let me start off by saying that Tadow is lucky that the only person that got caught up was Lee and not the both of them. They were told not to move the weight, but they did. They were doing too much and running their mouths in the process. Real niggas know not to put shit out there knowing there is competition all around. Niggas is hungry out there and they aren't eating. Of course they were going to go after who they thought were the weakest links. They were moving alone with no protection. All my guys roll deep. Tadow and Lee thought that the little money they were making out there with the product they were pushing was doing something. This isn't the same," T Ski explained. He could see that he had Mo's full attention and he was following along to everything that came from his mouth. "I hate that we lost our cousin and niggas are definitely going to pay for that," T Ski said.

"What about Bella?" Mo questioned. This was the most important information that he needed to know right now.

"Bro, are you sure you want to know what your baby mother has been up to?" T Ski questioned. He knew that once he revealed some of Bella secrets to Mo, he might not be able to handle them.

"What secrets could Bella have been keeping from me? We had a great relationship and we told each other everything," Mo admitted.

"Mo, Bella has another man thinking that Xavier is his son. Bella has been messing with some nigga name Dogg for the same amount of time she's been fucking with you," T Ski confessed. Mo stood there in disbelief. He knew that T Ski had to be making this up.

"Bella wouldn't do no shit like that to me. I took care of her and gave her a place to call home. I know that Xavier is my son. Where the fuck are you coming up with all of this bullshit from?" Mo wasn't believing a word T Ski said. In his mind, it was impossible for Bella to be playing him.

"I don't have a reason to lie to you, bro. I wasn't the one that tried to kill her. It was Dogg. I showed up at the apartment because I knew that he was going to see her. I wanted to make sure that she was good. There was no false entry because he had a key to the apartment. Bella was trying to break things off with him but he wasn't having it. She was more of an asset for him," T Ski explained.

"Why the fuck are you lying to me, T Ski? This shit can't be true. Yo, what the fuck is going on with motherfuckers I love and trust. Is anyone really loyal to me? I'm the last to know shit about what's going on in my own fucking relationship. I don't understand how you could know all of this shit and hold it in without mentioning anything to me. That's fucked up man." Mo was angry. He had to control his emotions knowing there were other men in the apartment. He didn't want anyone to think that he was soft.

"Bro, I just found out about this myself. You would be in jail right now had you known anything Bella was caught up in. I was trying to protect you," T Ski shared.

"How the fuck were you trying to protect me? Had this nigga not shot her, as you claim, I still wouldn't know that this bitch was doing me wrong. She was fucking some dirty ass nigga out here and you held that from me while supposing to be protecting me. Does that shit sound sane to you? How long have you been keeping this information from me?" T Ski stared at his brother. He knew that Mo wasn't going to be able to handle hearing what Bella was up to.

"The night the both of you argued. Remember, I told you she still had her earpiece in. I heard her talking to the dude."

Mo gave T Ski a dirty look. He still should've told him all that he had heard.

"Mo, this is exactly why I didn't tell you shit. We can't pull shit off with you going through your emotions over her. I was hoping that after everything was all done and said, the truth about her would've come out. I have too much shit going down right now, bro, for me to lose you because you aren't focused. This will have to be dealt with at another time. I need you to get your head back on straight so we can get shit popping. Bella is signing herself out of the hospital because she can't afford those expenses but she's going to need you. I got you, bro, all I'm asking from you is that you trust me and let me do me. I promise you, everything is going to unfold and turn out for our good," T Ski said with confidence.

Mo turned his head away, lost in his thoughts. At this point, he didn't have anything to lose. If what his brother had revealed to him was true, he definitely wanted his revenge.

"She's not getting my son. Bella got some random nigga staking claims on my son that he can give two shits about. I don't want him around her. I won't be able to rest knowing that she's going to come for him once she's released from the hospital. I can't let that shit happen. If dude tried to kill her before, he's going to try it again, but not with my son around to witness it," Mo stated.

"I got that taken care of. Are you good?" T Ski questioned.

"I'm good," Mo replied.

"I want to show you something. Let's go." T Ski moved toward the door. He exited the room with Mo following closely behind. T Ski walked across the hall into the room Mo had passed where the big machine was. "This is how K2O is being made. I put some of the chemicals I came up with in this tank and the machine mixes it and produces these contents," T Ski shared as he pointed to the different objects on the machine as he explained them to Mo.

"This shit is crazy," Mo said as he looked on and watched the machine produce the product.

"Listen, Mo, I have to leave Brooklyn for a while. I have a few things that I have to take care of. Pop is home now and things are going to go much easier for us. I have this big meeting tomorrow with the government about some of the technology I produced for them. Things is about to get live out here and I need to know that you're going to be able to handle things until I get back," T Ski retorted.

"Where are you going? How do you start something and then just up and leave? This was your idea and now you're trying to put me in charge of running things when I don't know what the hell it is that you got going on," Mo remarked.

"This was the reason for me having you to meet me at this location. I'm going to tell you everything you need to know and give you the whole run down of the operation so you will know how to run things with ease," T Ski explained.

"How long are you leaving for?" Mo asked.

"Two days." Although T Ski hated lying, he couldn't tell his brother the truth. He knew that Mo would probably back out and he needed him right now.

"I got you. I hope this shit don't blow up in my face. We got one cousin dead already. I don't want to lose my life or have anyone else in our family dying over no bullshit," Mo groped his chin. He couldn't help but to worry. He felt better knowing that T Ski was around and running shit himself, being that he was the one that started this shit.

"The family is going to be fine. Let's go in the kitchen and talk," T Ski retorted.

Sonovia Alexander

Chapter 12

Langston Hughes

"Did you get word yet about Tadow's whereabouts?" DC questioned Panama.

"Nah. Trust me, he's gon be out here tonight trying to find out who's responsible for his brother getting hit up," Panama replied. Panama inhaled on the cigarette he was smoking and blew smoke out of his nose and mouth. A knock came at the door, alarming both Panama and DC.

Panama stood from the couch and proceeded out of the living room toward the front door. Panama looked out the peep hole before unlocking the door.

"What's good, nigga? Where DC at?" Dogg asked.

"He's in the living room. Come in, nigga, and lock the door behind you."

Dogg did as he was told and moved toward the living room to go rap with DC.

"What's the word?" DC asked once Dogg entered the living room.

Dogg pulled out a plastic bag from inside his pants and opened it up. He poured the contents on the small table that was in the center of the floor.

DC's eyes lit up when he saw what had to be K2O. "This shit looks like weed," DC stated.

"I got the inside scoop on this shit and I had one of my people copycat that shit. This is K2O," Dogg said, pulling out a small vile with white contents inside.

"Do you drink this shit or what?" DC asked as he took the vile out of Dogg's hand, getting a closer look at it.

"Once you pour this shit out, it hardens up. You then chop that shit up as if it was crack and you smoke the shit or snort it," Dogg explained.

"How the fuck do you know so much about this shit and no one else does?" DC questioned.

"Remember my ex bitch, Bella, she knows someone that supplies the shit and was telling me everything," Dogg confessed.

"I want to see this bitch and ask her myself. I can't believe that a nigga like you got access to a drug that out of town niggas are pushing over here and no one else does. That shit don't add up my nigga. I know I told yawl motherfuckers to find out what's going on in the streets, but I didn't think that you would be the first to be put on," DC stated.

"I always come through and I been trying to show you that for a minute now. I had to kill that bitch. She started getting worried that her informants were going to find out that she was the one giving me the info. She got scared and stopped telling me shit. I showed up to the bitch crib unexpectedly and she got crazy on me. I didn't want niggas knowing that I was the one she was giving the information to, so she had to go," Dogg shared.

"So what the fuck is this other shit? How do you copycat something if you don't know what the fuck they are mixing in the shit to have it form into a rock from liquid?" DC couldn't believe that Dogg had the answers they were all seeking. Dogg wasn't a big timer and he didn't pull in as much money as DC's other workers, so it was hard for DC to believe that he was affiliated with anyone that knew about K2O.

"I told you, I got my peoples to copycat the shit. They know what they're doing. I guarantee you, if you put this shit out, fiends will be talking about this shit. We can charge a cheaper price for it, too. K2O is thirty dollars a pop. We can charge twenty dollars. DC you gotta trust me, son," Dogg stated.

DC didn't have anything to lose by allowing Dogg the chance to show him that this product would make them all money.

"Panama, go out with this nigga and let Fox try that shit out. I want you to let me know if it's something they will get hooked to. I'm not about to put my niggas on to no weak shit," DC explained. "Take that nigga to the spot and try it out and see what the results are. And if it's good, we can do business," DC shared.

Panama escorted Dogg out and led him to the first floor in the same building. Panama reached in his pocket for a key to unlock one of the apartment doors. There was a fiend name Fox that shared the apartment with his wife. Fox allowed Panama and DC the usage of his apartment to hold drugs, weapons, or anything else they needed to hide, in exchange for drugs.

Panama entered the apartment with Dogg following behind him. Panama immediately covered his nose from the stench coming from the inside of the apartment.

"Yo, Fox, where you at and what the fuck is that smell?" Panama called out. It was a mixture of ammonia and shit. Fox came from the back room dressed in a robe with nothing underneath. He was a tall slinky looking guy. He was dark as night and had a clean shaven head.

"Sorry about that, man. I had a little accident. I'm going to get that smell out of here in a minute," Fox stated.

Panama shook his head as he turned up his nose. He held his hand open for Dogg to pass him the product. Dogg placed a small bag in Panama's hand. Panama then tossed it in Fox's direction.

"This is some new shit I want you to try for me," Panama said.

Fox's eyes lit up as if he was a kid getting a gift from Santa himself. Fox hurried into the kitchen to sample the new drug. He opened it up and emptied the contents on the table. Fox drew back from the smell of what looked like weed to him.

"Why does it smell like that?" Fox questioned.

"Nigga, it can't smell no worse than this fucking apartment. I have shit to do, nigga, so try the shit or give it back," Panama stated with an attitude.

"No, I'll try it." Fox grabbed a small packet of bamboo paper. He took two small white sheets out and licked them together. He gathered the contents on the table and swept them onto the paper. He proceeded to roll the paper, not dropping a bit of the drugs inside. He then grabbed his lighter and sparked it up. Fox inhaled the contents and blew out the smoke. He immediately started to cough. He took another long and hard pull, inhaling and exhaling the smoke out of his nose. He repeated this until it was a small stem left of the paper he had rolled up.

"How is it?" Panama asked impatiently. He was ready to get out of the apartment before he vomited. He couldn't keep holding his breath because he was getting light headed in the process.

"You got some more?" Fox asked.

"Nigga, I asked you a fucking question? Is the shit good or not? You could be just asking for more because you're fucking thirsty," Panama shouted.

"It's real good. I need some more of that," Fox said with a nervous chuckle.

"I'll leave you another one but make sure that you put out the word that I got some new shit that is fire," Panama grabbed another bag from Dogg and tossed it to Fox. "Don't forget to spread the word. I'll holla at you later." Panama was relieved to be leaving from inside of the apartment. He and Dogg both headed back upstairs to report to DC.

Dogg had been praying that what he had put together would be just as good as the real stuff. Dogg had known Bella for a few years and used to fuck her for money. He knew the predicament she was in and he used it against her. Dogg had feelings for Bella but knew that she was sprung on Mo. Dogg had lost contact with

Bella when she left Brownsville. When he got word that she was back in the hood with a kid, Dogg went to see her.

Bella had wised up from the last time he had seen her. She was acting brand new like she was the shit. Dogg had a problem with that. He didn't possess the same control over her that he once had. When he had finally caught up to Bella while walking alone into her apartment, he snuck up behind her and placed his hand over her mouth so she wouldn't scream. Bella was petrified and tried to maneuver her way out of the tight hold he had on her. Dogg whispered in her ear for her not to scream as he loosened his grip on her. Bella nodded her head in agreement, trying to calm herself down.

Dogg grilled Bella for a few minutes, asking her question after question. Bella never gave him the response he was looking for and, before he could do anything that she thought he would regret, she told him that it was a possibility that her son was his. Dogg didn't believe her for one minute. He figured she tossed that in the air because she was afraid he was going to fuck her up. He was glad that she came around and started talking, knowing he wouldn't leave her alone. Bella hadn't slept with him in a few years but that didn't stop her from giving him information to step his street game up.

Bella knew that Dogg was a small timer looking to come up. Bella had sources because at one point in her life, she lived on the streets. She knew a lot of things and Dogg knew that she was beneficial to him. Dogg was hyped when she had told him about K2O. Dogg knew about it before it had even spread through the projects.

Dogg had been waiting for the day that he would come up and today was that day. He knew that this would put him right on top where he belonged. He was ready to take over DC's territory but just needed to get in good with him so he could watch his every move. Dogg was about to be on top and he was willing to do whatever he had to in order to build his brand.

He was unsure of how and why Bella was giving him all the information he needed, but he was glad that she did. He didn't want to kill her but he couldn't let her live. Dogg knew that he would have a lot of problems and he didn't need that kind of heat right now if Bella flipped on him.

Chapter 13

May 19, 2005
Tilden Projects

Mo unlocked the door to the apartment and entered. He was hoping that everyone would be asleep. It was almost 4am. He was exhausted. Mo moved about in the house, trying not to awaken anyone. When he strode passed his mother's room, he saw that the door was closed. Mo went to turn the knob when he remembered that his father was home. Mo continued on past his mother's room and entered his bedroom that he now shared with Xavier.

Xavier was sound asleep. Mo kicked off his sneakers and pulled off his shirt, tossing it intp the hamper that was next to his dresser. Mo crawled into bed beside his son and closed his eyes. T Ski had filled him in on so much and he tried his best to remember everything. He was glad that T Ski had someone that would be helping him keep afloat of things. Mo knew that there were going to be plenty of sleepless nights to pull off everything T Ski had planned. Mo rolled over to his side and pulled Xavier in close to him. He held his son tight. The thought of losing his son crossed his mind. Mo couldn't let that happen.

Mo removed his arm from Xavier and sat up in the bed. He couldn't sleep until he spoke to Bella. He had to make sure that he made it clear to her that she would never get his son as long as she had some stupid ass nigga after her. Mo knew that his relationship was over, but he wanted to know why Bella lied to him.

Mo grabbed his phone as he climbed out of bed and walked around toward the window. He cracked it open and sat down on the fold-up chair he had in the room. Mo dialed Bella's number. He was going to leave her a message, knowing she was probably asleep. He had to make it clear to her that he knew everything and the only way she would get Xavier from him was to take him to court. Mo peeked over at Xavier and watched his son sleep. *There is no way in hell that anyone other than me could be his father,* he thought. Xavier looked just like him and, on top of that, if he was a genius like his uncle, he had to be Mo's blood.

Mo held the phone up to his ear after dialing Bella's number. He didn't know exactly what he was going to say, but he had to let her know that if she tried taking his son from him, he was going to kill her.

"Why are you calling me so early in the morning?" Bella asked.

Mo didn't expect her to answer but figured the doctors or nurses were probably making their rounds.

"I need to talk to you about something important. I was just planning on leaving you a message. Since I have you on the phone, do you want to tell me why you lied to me about my brother being the one trying to kill you? You forgot to tell me that you have been fucking a dude name Dogg who believes he might be my son's father. I find out that this nigga tried to kill you and you pin it on my brother, who was probably there to save your damn life. You can forget about coming here to get my son. He's not going anywhere with you. Don't think about going back to the apartment because I changed the locks to the door last night." Mo tried to whisper but he was getting upset thinking about the betrayal from the one woman he had loved and gave the world to.

"Mo, I wasn't fucking Dogg. It's been years since I been with him. I don't know how you found out about that, but it's not what you think," Bella explained. She thought that if she turned everything on T Ski, she would be able to get Mo to turn away from his family and give her and Xavier the life they deserved. Bella didn't think things all the way through. She just knew in her mind that Mo wasn't going to give up on her that easily and would come chasing after her and their son. Bella knew that wasn't going to happen now.

She didn't think about what Dogg would do if he found out that he didn't kill her. He was coming back to finish what he started. Bella hated that she had given up so much information to Dogg, but she did it to save her family. She wanted to go back to the life her and Mo shared before coming back to Brownsville.

"Why did you lie on my brother, Bella? T Ski loved you like a sister. Why would you try and turn me against my own brother?" Mo was hurt and never thought that she would betray him like this.

"I just wanted my family back, Mo. I wanted you to see how your life would be without me and Xavier. I didn't mean to do this to you or your family. I'm sorry," Bella said. She knew that she needed Mo now more than ever. He was now taking her home away from her and if Dogg found out that she was still alive, he was going to kill her. Bella felt stupid and should've followed her fist instincts to tell Mo about Dogg and let him take care of him. Now she was in deeper than she wanted to be with no protection. Her parents couldn't protect her like Mo could. She had to make sure now that Mo or T Ski found out that she had given up information to Dogg.

"I can't fuck with a bitch like you. I'm done and you better stay the fuck away from my son." Mo disconnected the call. He was done talking and done listening. He knew that Bella required more time from him but to go through all that to get his attention was messed up. Mo tossed his phone on to his dresser and headed back over to his bed. He climbed in and laid on his back. He was in deep thought as he placed both his hands behind his head. Mo knew he needed to get some sleep because in a couple of hours, shit was about to turn up.

***

Downstate Hospital

Bella sat up in her bed holding her phone in hand. She couldn't believe that Mo had hung up on her. This was turning out to be a disaster. *Mo wasn't supposed to give up on me that easily,* she thought. *He was supposed to love me wholeheartedly.*

Bella didn't know how he found out about Dogg, but she was glad that he didn't know everything about what the two of them were up to or she would be dead. Dogg wouldn't have to come finish the job because Mo would kill her himself. Bella hated herself for fucking up the one good thing she had going on in her life. She just wanted Mo to keep a clear path and not get associated in what T Ski had going on. She didn't want to lose him to the streets or have her son grow up without his father. She had her reasons behind her actions.

Bella dialed her friend's number. She couldn't let this man get away from her. She loved Mo and wasn't about to give the next woman the satisfaction of reaping all the good he had to offer.

"Hello," Nancy answered in a sleepy voice.

"I'm sorry to wake you, boo. I need to talk to you," Bella said.

"Oh my God, Bella. I have been trying to find out where the hell you were. I went to the hospital and they said you had been moved. I been so worried about you. Tina had told me everything and I thought your ass was dead, bitch. Where the fuck are you?" Nancy questioned while crawling out of bed.

"I'm at Downstate. I have to discharge myself because I don't have enough money to stay in here and get the treatment I need. I'm going to be alright though," Bella explained.

"I heard you were shot. Do you know who did this to you?" Nancy asked.

"I'll talk to you about that later. I was shot in my arm and the bullet luckily went through. It missed my lungs by a few inches. I would've been worse off had it hit my lungs. They have been keeping me medicated because I had a concussion. I hit my head hard on Xavier's race car bed, and then to the floor I went, hitting it again. I'm lucky that they kept my ass in here this long. I was told that my doctor bills were being covered and then when I was moved by my parents, they told me that I wasn't covered," Bella revealed.

"Damn, that's fucked up. When are you discharging yourself?" Nancy asked.

"In a few hours. I'm waiting until my doctor gets back so I can speak to him. After I see him, I'm out of here. I need a favor though."

"What's up, ma?"

"I need to crash at your place until I get on my feet. Shit is fucked up right now for me. Mo isn't fucking with me because I did some foul shit and now I got another nigga out there thinking that he killed me and I don't need that nigga to find out that I'm alive and catch up to me. I was going to my parents' house but he would be able to get at me if I touch down in Brownsville. He got niggas on the lookout and I'm not fucking with over there," Bella shared.

"I got you, boo. I can't believe that Mo wouldn't still have your back no matter what you did. He's still your baby father and you his baby mother. That's fucked up that he's turning his back on you at a time like this." Nancy was upset but didn't know the real reason why Mo didn't want any dealings with Bella.

"I have a lot to put you on to when I get out of here. Would you be able to pick me up from here?" Bella asked.

"I'll be there. Hit my phone and let me know before you get out of there so I can be there before hand."

"Thanks, Nancy. I owe you big time. I'll see you in a few hours." Bella ended the call. She was glad that her friend was opening up her place for her to rest her head until she figured out what her next move would be.

Chapter 14

Langston Hughes

"Nigga. It's 9am. Where the fuck are you?" DC shouted into the phone.

"I'm outside the door. Open up and let me in," Dogg stated.

DC ended the call and walked over to the door. He looked through the peep hole and saw that Dogg was alone. He unlocked the door and let Dogg inside. Dogg entered the apartment handing a big duffle bag to DC while passing him.

"How much?" DC asked.

"Twenty-fie," Dogg answered.

"Twenty-five? Nigga, that's a little steep don't you think for something that's not 100%?" DC remarked with attitude.

"I was up all night with my people putting that shit together. I can get you more but this need to move first and fast. I need the dough to re-up and get more shit," Dogg answered. He was ready to dead DC on his whole operation because he was a stingy ass nigga.

"Panama, get the dough for this nigga. I'm telling your ass now, this shit better move or we will have a problem," DC threatened.

"It will move, son, I'm telling you. It's Friday and you already know its payday. Now is the time to have niggas go hard and make this paper. I bet in a few hours this shit will be gone and you're going to want more of it," Dogg said with confidence.

"Let me be the judge of that," DC replied.

Panama passed DC a medium sized brown paper bag full of cash. DC handed it over to Dogg. Dogg opened the bag and peeked inside.

"I'm about to get back in the lab and keep this shit coming," Dogg shared before opening up the door and exiting the apartment.

Dogg skipped three to five steps trying to get out of the building. He had to get ghost and start building his own camp away from DC. Dogg had given him some product, but it wasn't what he had given him the night before. The product looked identical to what he had showed DC last night, but it wouldn't give other fiends the same effect it gave Fox. Dogg knew what he was about to start and he was prepared. He had his own team now and he was about to be the big man in the streets that everyone came to.

"You good, son?" Ace asked Dogg when he reached the outside of the building.

Dogg was sweating like he was being chased by someone. Ace gripped his .45 he had in his pocket. He was ready to set shit off if there was a problem.

"I'm good, son. We need to move now. Let's go meet up with your people so we can get this shit popping," Dogg stated as he started walking down the street with Ace following closely behind him.

***

Bed Stuy
Halsey Street

"Damn, Bella. What the fuck was you thinking? I see why he don't want any parts of you. You have to fix that shit some kind of way to get your man back," Nancy stated.

"He doesn't know the half of it and I'm afraid to tell him. I don't fear Dogg more than I fear Mo. That nigga is straight crazy. I know he would kill me if he knew all the shit I have done. I just wanted my man back. Mo stayed off the streets for a few years and I just wanted to keep things that way. We have a son that needs his father. He saw how the streets destroyed his father," Bella explained.

"His father is home now, you said. Bella, girl I don't even know what to say to you about this shit. You fucked up big time. I wonder what Mo would do if he found out who the person was that was giving you all the info to share with Dogg."

Nancy felt bad for her girl but also thought that Bella was stupid as hell for what she had done. Good men were hard to find and she had one of the good ones. Nancy knew that it would break Mo's heart if he learned the truth about who gave up all of their plans.

"I don't want to think about this shit right now. I have to make sure that I get back in good with Mo. He won't return my phone calls. I called him three times and left him messages. This nigga is pissed, but I have to see him." Bella hoped that she would be able to win Mo back, but she was worried that he wouldn't accept her. She hated rejection.

"You need to stay your ass in this house and get some rest. If you still want to go and see Mo tomorrow, I'll take you to see him myself. Right now I think you need to stay put and think things through on how you're going to approach him. You do know that eventually, you will have to tell him everything. Don't hold no information back because it's going to fuck you in the long run." Nancy knew that telling lies always found a way to catch back up to you. She had been through her share of drama in her life with men but never as bad as what Bella was experiencing.

"I need to call my mother. I'm glad that she had gone by my apartment a few days ago and collected some of my things. I just need to get them from her so I can have something to put on. Damn, she has my bag with my wallet inside, too," Bella sighed.

"Girl, stop worrying yourself. I want you to get some rest and take your mind off all the shit you got going on. You know your ass can't afford to be back up in the hospital so I'm going to need you to chill before one of those migraines come on. I don't have anything strong enough here to help you cope with pain so chill out, girl."

Bella nodded her head in agreement. She leaned back on the pillows as she made herself comfortable in the bed. Nancy had a nice and cozy two bedroom apartment. She was the only friend Bella had that was single and lived alone with enough room to accommodate her for a few days.

"I don't need a migraine right now. I'm going to get some rest. Thanks again for your hospitality," Bella said while yawning.

"No problem. I'll be in my room if you need me," Nancy said as she stood from the bed and headed out of the room toward her own bedroom.

***

Tilden Projects

"What's going on, son? How are you feeling this morning?" Po asked Taz as he walked into the kitchen where Taz B sat eating cold cereal.

"I'm good, pops. How did you and Uncle Gus get out?" Taz B knew that T Ski had to be the one behind it but wasn't sure.

"Son, I wish I had the answers. I'm just glad to be home. Your mother and I talked all night long. Why didn't you guys get her to another doctor? What kind of meds has she been taking that is all of a sudden making her feel like herself again?" Po questioned. He had fallen asleep before he could speak with Mo.

"Pop, she didn't want to go. We couldn't force her to do something against her will. T Ski has been giving her something to help her with pain, I believe. I'm not really sure what it is."

Taz wasn't sure what T Ski had been giving his mother but it had to be working since she was getting out of bed and speaking.

He was glad his father was home. This was now as good a time as any to move on with his life and not have to worry about his mother being looked after.

"Evelyn shared some things with me about T Ski last night. Do you care to tell me what's been going on since I've been gone?" Po asked.

Mo walked into the kitchen before Taz could answer his father.

"Good morning," Mo spoke.

"Good morning. You're up early and I know you got in pretty late. Where you been?" Po questioned.

Mo smiled at his father. He felt like a twelve year old being questioned as if he'd missed his curfew.

"I was out with T Ski handling some things," Mo replied.

"Where is he? He's the man that I need to be having a sit down with," Po suggested.

"He's not here. He won't be home for another two days," Mo mentioned.

"That nigga is only sixteen. Who the hell gave him permission to stay out the house for two days?" Po scolded.

"Pop, he had important things to do and a few meetings he had to attend. T Ski knows how to handle himself," Mo retorted.

"Hold the fuck up. What kind of meetings do a sixteen year old attend without an adult? I want to know what's going on with my kids. I don't know how shit was while I was away, but I'm home now. Call your brother and tell him I want to see him," Po ordered.

Mo didn't say a word. He had held things down all these years while his father was away and he would be lying to himself if he said that he didn't feel some type of way. Mo had stepped up and took care of his brothers and he knew that it might be messed up but he couldn't help thinking that his father had no right to question what had gone down since he'd been away. Mo thought he did a good job taking care of his family.

"I'll try to reach him," Mo said.

"No. Don't try. You tell him I want him home today," Po shouted.

Mo stood face to face with his father. He wanted to say something but knew better than to go up against his father. Mo maneuvered around his father and headed back toward his bedroom. While passing his mother's slightly ajar door, he could see that she didn't have a shirt on. Chills ran up Mo's spine. He didn't want to entertain the thought of his parent's possibly having sex. He knew that it was going to be soon time for him to go. He was glad that his pops was home for his mother's sake but Mo knew they were going to need their privacy.

Mo entered his bedroom. Xavier was just waking up.

"Good morning, sleepy head. Why don't you go into the kitchen and make you a bowl of cereal after you brush your teeth and wash your face, okay," Mo said as he picked up his cell phone.

"Good morning, daddy, and ok." Xavier exited the room.

Mo noticed that he had a few missed calls coming from Bella. She had left him a voicemail. He would listen to it later but he had to try and reach T Ski. Mo hoped he would answer the phone. He knew that T Ski had an important conference this morning. He was unsure of the time but he was going to try his luck anyway.

"What's up, Mo?" T Ski answered on the first ring.

"Pop just went off on me. He wants you home right now. I don't know what to tell him, man. I think maybe you should call the house and speak to him or something," Mo explained.

T Ski smirked over the phone. He was glad his brother couldn't see his face right now. T Ski could tell that Mo wasn't happy about his pops giving him orders. T Ski had his house bugged and could hear everything going on inside his house.

"I'm on my way to the house now anyway. I'll talk to him then," T Ski said.

"I thought you were going out of town for two days," Mo questioned.

"I'm still going. I just got out of this meeting a few minutes ago. I'm stopping by the house to holla at pops and then I'll be on my way. Don't worry, Mo, I'll take care of everything," T Ski assured him.

Mo disconnected the call. He was trying to contain his anger. Flashes of his mother and father having sex crept through his mind. They were still married but Mo didn't like the fact that his father would take it there with his mother knowing that she wasn't out of the woods yet. She was up and talking but that still didn't mean anything.

Mo tossed his phone onto the bed. He got down on his hands and knees preparing himself to do a small workout. He was stressed and needed to relieve some of it. Mo did one hundred pushups, working up a sweat. When he was done, he laid on his back and started doing sit ups. After about fifty sit ups, Mo was tempted to stop until he started thinking about Bella. He continued his sets as he felt the pain rip through his body. It had been a while since he had worked out. There was so much going on in his life and he had to get it back on track for his son's sake. Po walked into the room and stood over Mo. Mo stopped his workout. He stared up at his father. Po extended his hand to help Mo from the floor. Mo took it and got up from the floor.

Mo had sweat pouring down his face as he stood face to face, staring at the man that gave him life. Po and Mo could pass for twins. Mo felt like he was staring in the mirror at himself.

"I'm sorry about yelling at you in there. I know you have been the man of the house for the last few years. I was wrong for that. Thank you for being the man you have become. After talking to your uncles last night, there's a lot of shit going on that I need to know about. It seems like the only one that has all the answers I need is your brother. I don't think he should be staying out all crazy and he's only sixteen. There's too much going on in the hood and I'm not trying to lose any of my kids to the streets," Po explained.

Mo nodded his head in agreement.

"He's on his way home. Anything you need to know, I'm sure he will have more answers for you than he had for me," Mo said.

"What's that supposed to mean?" Po questioned.

"T Ski will fill you in on what's been going on in the hood," Mo replied.

Po stepped out of Mo's room when he heard someone unlocking the front door. Po saw T Ski enter the apartment, locking the door behind him.

"I guess I will find out now," Po said before exiting Mo's room. "Let me talk to you, T," Po said.

T Ski headed toward the back where his father stood.

"Let's go in my room, pop," T Ski said as he unlocked his bedroom door and held it open.

Mo could see from the door of his bedroom how empty T Ski's room looked. He wondered when and how T Ski got everything out of his room without anyone knowing. Mo couldn't get a better look because Po had closed the door. Mo shook his head. He knew that things were going to be a lot different since his father was home. The only difference was, he came home to men and not little boys. Po was in for a rude awakening once he found out who his son really was.

Mo headed for the kitchen to check on Xavier. He wanted to make sure his kid was good. Taz was getting ready to leave for work. Mo looked at his brother, thinking about what had transpired between him and T Ski. Mo could only pray that nothing bad would happen to Taz because T Ski would definitely have a problem if it did happen.

Sonovia Alexander

Chapter 15

Langston Hughes

"DC, what time are you planning on leaving?" Cruise asked.

"I just gave the work to my boys. Panama out right now collecting the rest of my money, and then we can head out. I hope you got shit set up," DC said to his brother.

"Nigga, what the fuck you think I been doing down there all those damn days. Niggas don't have time for no fucking vacations. I got the business taken care of. All I need is for you to go meet up with these damn investors so we can open up this spot," Cruise explained.

"Did you go check up on my shit while you were out there? I haven't been home in a minute," DC shared.

"Everything is cool," Cruise remarked.

"Good. My camp should be good until I get back Monday. I'm hoping this shit bring in the dough that I copped from Dogg." DC was hoping that he had made a wise decision.

"When did you start copping work from Dogg punk ass?" Cruise questioned.

"Didn't you get my text, nigga? I explained the shit to you last night," DC said in defense.

"I was fucked up. I didn't pay that shit no mind. You trust that nigga like that?"

DC was becoming annoyed. He didn't like his brother questioning his moves when Cruise worked for him too.

"Nigga, it ain't about trust. It's about my paper. If Fox said the shit was good, then I will take that nigga word for it. These out of town niggas is taking over and I need to make sure my shit is secure. If the cash flow stop, we can't upkeep this damn club we're about to invest in," DC stated. Cruise shook his head but didn't respond. "I'll wait downstairs for Panama. Lock up the place so we can get out of here." DC opened the door and proceeded out of the apartment.

***

Tilden Projects

"Are you fucking with me right now?" Po asked his son. The shit T Ski had just informed him had blown his mind. There was no way that T Ski could've been the one that got him and his brother off. Finding out that his sixteen year old was a damn genius and was calling all the shots was fucking Po's head up.

"Pop, I'm not lying to you. I have a lot that needs to be done in a short time span. I need for you and your brothers to get back on your old school status. I haven't touched a few projects yet because I needed you and Uncle Gus home first. I gave Mo the rundown of the whole operation last night. He knows exactly what has to be done. Pop, no one can know that it's me behind this or it will mess everything up," T Ski retorted.

"I'm your father. I would never let you go down for anything. If you're sure that you got this, and I can be involved to make sure that everything goes accordingly, let's make it happen. One thing that needs to be done first. I'm not leaving your mother and sister here. They don't need to be in Brooklyn if all of this is going down."

T Ski smiled. He had a place for his family already but knew that he wouldn't be able to get his mother to leave Brooklyn unless his father asked her to leave. T Ski would be at ease knowing that his family was out of Brooklyn. He had already had his uncle take Tadow and Sheryl out of Brooklyn. He needed his family gone, too. His grandmother was good, along with their other family members, because they had no parts of what T Ski had going on.

"I got that covered but I don't know if mommy is going to be up to leaving," T Ski confessed.

"You leave your mother up to me. When can we get them out of here?" Po asked.

"As soon as you can convince her that it's time to go," T Ski admitted.

"Say no more. One more thing. What's this I hear about you wishing death upon your brother? What the fuck is that about?" Taz B had made sure to tell his father how his youngest son felt about him.

"I was pissed at him, but he knows I didn't mean it. He doubted that any of this would work and he blamed me for what happened to Lee. I just exploded because I was hurt and mad at the same time. I'll talk to him. I have somewhere I need to be. If you can get mommy to leave today, I need to make sure that everything is good over there," T Ski shared.

"We are definitely getting her out of here today. I don't know if I like the idea of you traveling alone. I know that you're smart and all that other stuff, but you're still a kid," Po confessed.

"I'm good pops. I have people with me at all times. Here, take this phone. I'll call you in two hours top and hopefully she will be ready to go," T Ski said before opening his door and exiting his room.

Po sat on the bed as he watched his youngest son walk out on him. Po was disappointed in himself for all the years he had missed out on with his kids and wife. He was glad to be home now but things just seemed different. He was still unsure of what was going on with his wife and now his youngest son was trying to take over Brooklyn, pushing a new drug that he invented himself. Po had taught his boys that family values meant the world to him and had installed it in them. He knew that T Ski would make sure that when he accomplished all of his goals, his family was going to be alright. Po vowed that he would die to make everything T Ski had planned pay off because jail wasn't an option for him. He didn't ever plan on going back.

***

Plaza Projects

"Yo, isn't those the two right there, boss," Mecca said to T Ski.

T Ski looked over in the direction where Mecca was pointing. He spotted Drew and Cali sitting on a bench. T Ski smiled.

"Pablo, pull the car over. Mecca, get Chase on the line and tell him not to move. I got this," T Ski said as he pulled his baseball cap from out of the back seat of the car and placed it on his head. T Ski reached under his seat, grabbed a .45, and held it in his hand. Mecca looked around to make sure there were no police in sight.

T Ski stepped out of the car and walked around toward the sidewalk. He placed his hand inside his pocket and walked in the direction where Drew and Cali were. T Ski knew that the three car loads full of armed men were waiting for the chance to get out and protect their boss. Drew was spitting a rhyme while Cali sat beside him bopping his head to the sound of Drew's words. T Ski was a few feet away from them when he looked up and checked his surroundings. There were no witnesses in sight as he continued on his path.

T Ski walked past the two to see if they noticed someone approaching them, but they were in tune with what they were doing. T Ski looked around once again before turning around and walking up behind both men. T Ski pulled his gun out and let off four shots hitting them both in the back of their heads. T Ski picked up his pace as he walked off toward the truck. Pablo had already gotten out of the truck to open the door for T Ski. He quickly got inside the truck and Pablo drove off.

Drew and Cali laid slumped over on top of one another, never seeing their lives ending.

T Ski pulled off the hat and his shirt that had blood splattered over it. T Ski wiped his face and tossed the shirt in the back seat. He had on a white tee underneath his shirt. He felt better knowing that he had laid down the two responsible for killing his cousin.

"Pablo, head to the Stuy. I need to go get cleaned up real quick," T Ski ordered.

"Damn, boss, you know I could've handled that for you," Mecca said.

"That was personal." T Ski's response was short.

Mecca nodded his head. He had been rolling with T Ski for a little over a year. He respected the kid and he was down for him since he made sure his pockets were right.

Mecca had met T Ski through one of his nieces. Mecca had become fond of the young boy. He was going to grill T Ski at first because his niece was sixteen and he was the only male figure she had in her life. Before he could say anything to T Ski, he had approached him.

"Hey, I'm Terence. You must be Mecca. Kya talks about you all the time," T Ski said extending his hand for Mecca to shake. Mecca shook his head as he gave T Ski a pound.

"Yes. That's my baby right there. How old are you?" Mecca questioned.

"I'm fifteen. We go to the same school. I have been telling her a few things about me and she told me that I should come and holla at you."

Mecca raised his brow. "Why would she suggest that you holla at me?" Mecca was curious and he was definitely going to have to talk to his niece.

"I would like for you to do business with me. I own my own company and I'm looking to expand and need the right kind of people to get on board with me. If you have the time, you can look over this contract and get back to me if interested. I need to get home but my number is on the bottom if you have any questions. It was nice meeting you and tell Kya I will see her in school tomorrow," T Ski had left the apartment hoping that Mecca would get down with him. Kya had told him a lot of stories about her uncle and that was the kind of nigga he wanted to have his back.

Mecca had looked the papers over and couldn't believe what the contract was for. T Ski wanted to hire him as a hitman. He thought the kid was crazy until he continued on reading. He was amazed at how the contents on the document were sought out. He grabbed his phone and stored T Ski's number inside. He was definitely going to see what this young boy was talking about. Mecca figured that he was working for someone but found out a week later that T Ski was the man in charge. Mecca envied the boys genius mind and wished that he could've put something like that together in his youthful days. He had become very close to T Ski and grew to love him as if he was his blood. He treated his niece like a queen and he could tell that she was in love with him.

Mecca normally would've kept his niece sheltered and away from boys, but there was something special about T Ski and not because of him being his boss. T Ski was family oriented and had told Mecca all about his mother. He knew that T Ski loved his family and that was a plus in his eyes. Mecca felt a bond between him and T Ski because he knew things about him that his own brothers didn't know. He never told his brothers that he had a girlfriend. He never told his brothers that he had niggas killed and was moving something he called K2O in four of the boroughs, Jersey, and it had even gotten inside the prisons.

T Ski shared everything with Mecca and told him that when he was ready to, he would bring his brothers on board. He had to make sure things were on point and he had the right amount of money flowing first before presenting this to him. He knew that T Ski mixed up the product himself inside his home and would do it in his apartment as well. Mecca was down for him. T Ski told Kya everything and in Mecca's mind, he knew that T Ski had to really love her to tell her his every move. Niggas in the hood didn't tell their girls what they were doing in the street. The less they knew, the better off they were.

Mecca was the one that had gotten all the connections from the guys out of town for T Ski. All he did was mention Mecca's name and niggas came running. Mecca knew some of these cats were the realest and about their paper. He knew they would be down.

"Keep the car running, Pablo, I'll only be a minute," T Ski said as he hopped out of the truck and took off in a light jog toward the building. He made it to the apartment in less than two minutes. T Ski headed inside and went straight toward the bathroom. Once he had washed himself off, he went inside the bedroom across from the bathroom and pulled a polo shirt out of his duffle bag. He placed the shirt on and exited the room. He nodded at his workers and kept it moving.

T Ski had to get a lot of things done. He was on a schedule because he was flying Kya out to Georgia in a few hours. She was leaving for college. T Ski was going to miss her but wanted her to get her education. He had tutored her to prepare her for her tests and she passed with high scores, getting her accepted to some of the best colleges. T Ski was paying for her tuition and knew that Kya was going to be the woman he married. He couldn't wait to introduce her to his family, but T Ski decided that would have to wait. He liked his privacy and didn't need the conviction from his brothers.

T Ski didn't like keeping things from his brothers but he knew they wouldn't have understood what he was trying to do. He had to make sure that he had things on lock before he could share anything with his family. The hardest thing T Ski ever had to do was tell his mother about his business. He told his mother everything that one night he went in her room to give her medicine. He didn't think she would approve but he was ecstatic when Mo had told him she gave her blessings. It made T Ski want to go harder. He had no choice at this point.

Sonovia Alexander

Chapter 16

Tilden Projects

"Bitch, knock on the door. Why the fuck are you acting all scared for?" Nancy asked.

"Shut up, Nancy. I'm scared. I know I'm not even supposed to be coming to his mother house but he's not answering my phone calls," Bella stated nervously. She inhaled and knocked on the door before Nancy decided to leave her. There was someone always home at the apartment with his mother. She wanted Mo to be there, and then again, she didn't want him there. Bella didn't know what he would say to her once he saw her on the other side of the door.

Bella knocked again. She put her ear to the door to hear if she heard any movements but she didn't. "I don't know where they could be. Someone is always home with his mother. Where the hell is my son?"

Bella knocked on the door a little harder this time. She hoped nothing had happened to Mo's mother. Bella was concerned. She didn't have the slightest clue where any of them could be. She was ready to get the hell out of Brownsville before she ran into

Dogg. Knowing she didn't know where Mo could be, she had no protection.

"Girl, I'm ready to get the hell out of here. It's too many cops outside. No one is there. You're just going to have to keep calling this nigga until he answer. I don't feel safe over here," Nancy proclaimed.

"I don't either and was thinking the same damn thing. I'm ready."

Bella walked off heading toward the elevator. She pressed the button while retrieving her phone from her bag. She quickly dialed Mo's number again. The phone rang out before going to his voicemail. Bella shook her head. She couldn't blame him for ignoring her because she had fucked up. She had even treated him fucked up while she was in the hospital. Bella decided to text him. He probably wouldn't answer this one, like he didn't answer the other twenty texts she'd sent him.

I'm at your house. Wanted to speak to you face to face but didn't get a response. Please call me.

Bella sent the message and hoped that Mo would text back this time. The elevator doors opened and both girls stepped inside. Bella pressed number one as the doors swung close. She kept looking down at her phone, hoping that Mo would text back.

She knew in her mind that it was wishful thinking but he was going to have to respond to her sooner or later. He had her son and he couldn't keep him from her.

They reached the first floor. The doors opened and Bella and Nancy both exited the elevators. Nancy screwed her face up at the sight of piss laying on the floor in front of the door.

"That is so fucking nasty. I hate the fucking projects. Mother-fuckers is just straight dirty over here. They should've pissed in the fucking corner if they couldn't make it to the damn bathroom," Nancy complained.

Bella giggled. She was used to this, being that she lived in the projects all her life. This was nothing new. Nancy pushed the door open and jumped over the piss trying not to bust her ass. She had on wedges and they were not meant to be jumping in.

Nancy couldn't wait to get from over here. She could see a few people running in a direction where a bunch of cops had the streets blocked off. Nancy knew that meant that someone had gotten shot or killed. She unlocked her car door and entered her vehicle. Bella jumped inside the car to as her phone beeped. She looked at the phone and saw that Mo had texted her back. She clicked on the message to open it and immediately frowned when she saw the two words Mo sent. "We moved," was his only response. Bella wanted to scream. He didn't mention anything about them moving. She thought back and knew that she didn't give him the chance to share anything with her. She was glad that he responded, but wanted more out of him.

Nancy pulled off while Bella continued to fish for information. She started sending texts to Mo but he wasn't responding to any of them. She guessed that he only responded so she wouldn't show back up at his mom's crib. Bella was getting agitated and could feel a headache coming on. She sat her phone on her lap, leaned her head back on the seat, and closed her eyes. When he was ready, he would hit her back. She told him that she had something important to tell him but he still hadn't responded.

Bella forgot that he had told her over the phone that his cousin had died. She figured that was probably why he got his mother out of Brooklyn. Bella knew shit was going to get hot for them. She was afraid to entertain the things T Ski wanted her to do. It was sickening and she felt worse that Mo would even agree to her risking her life. She had her reasons to be mad with him as well. He thought she was cheating on him but that was far from the truth. It still puzzled her on how Mo found out about Dogg in the first place. He never ran into Dogg, he knew her whereabouts at all times, Xavier was never exposed to Dogg except for that one time. Bella hadn't told her son the nigga's name or anything about him for him to repeat to Mo.

She was eventually going to track him down, but until then, she was going to stay out of Brownsville.

***

Seth Low Projects
Later that day...

"Yo, that's my cousin right there I was telling you about. Yo, Ron, over here, my nigga," Ace shouted, getting Ron D's attention.

Ron D headed up the walkway to meet up with his cousin. He was surprised to hear from him, being that they lived in the same hood and barely saw one another.

"What's good, fam?" Ron D said, giving his cousin dap and a brotherly hug.

"I'm good, my dude. Yo, this is my nigga Dogg. He got put on to that new shit that these out of town niggas are pushing. Yo, you trying to get some of this paper or what? Let's go inside the building real quick," Ace offered. The guys headed inside of the building. They were posted up in the lobby.

"You already know I'm down. I been seeing a lot of these out of town niggas posting up pushing that shit. Those niggas roll deep. I roll for dolo, but if I'm gon be pushing that shit, I'm gon need some help moving it in Tilden," Ron D admitted.

"I got you covered. I just wanted to make sure that you were down. We got our soldiers ready for whatever. This is our fucking hood and I'm not about to sit there and let no fucking pretty boys stop me from getting my paper, you feel me?" Ace said.

"That's what's up. How did you get your hands on the shit?" Ron D questioned.

"My ex bitch, Bella, got me everything I needed to know. I duplicated the shit and my shit might be better than what they got out here. I just passed off a nice piece of some next shit just to get this 25g so I could cook up some more work. Ace said that you was a wild nigga and in order for us to get this paper, we gon catch a lot of static from some niggas out here, especially DC boys. Those niggas don't make no real money like DC. I was running for that nigga but he wasn't giving me half of what his brother was paying his team. I got that old bastard because that shit he got will have fiends going somewhere else for their shit.

When his boys start losing out on money, we gon have to move in on them niggas to take over their turf," Dogg babbled.

Ron D took in all that Dogg had shared. He knew the nigga was sleazy. He talked too much to niggas he didn't even know. Ron D saw right through him. He was a small timer who had thought he found his come up.

"That's what I'm talking about. I'm down for whatever, my nigga. You just let me know when to move and I'm there. Do you have some of the work on you? I want to see that shit," Ron D asked. He knew that he was dealing with a stupid ass nigga. Just as he thought, Dogg passed him a small bag. "This shit is official," Ron D said as he examined the contents inside the small bag.

"I already got some of my team pushing it out here. I'm going to have some for you in a few. We need to get this shit out there quick," Dogg stated.

"That's cool. Do you have a few more pieces on you? I know a few fiends by my way that I can sell this shit to and have them put the word out. I guarantee you, those thirsty motherfuckers will have niggas running over here," Ron D suggested.

"I told you my nigga would come through," Ace said with a crooked smile. Dogg took out a few more bags and passed it to Ron D.

"Yo, you want to ride with me back to my side and see how fast this shit go?" Ron D asked Ace.

"Nah. I'm about to set up shop in a minute as soon as my boys get here. I'm going to holla at you as soon as he get the work for you. I'll work your side with you later on tonight so I can link you up with some people," Ace said.

"Cool. Hit me up. I'll see yawl in a minute. Good looking, son," Ron D said to Dogg.

Ron D walked out of the building and proceeded back toward his building. Ron D waited until he was out of sight before pulling out his phone and sending Mo a 911 text. He knew that Mo and his family had left the building, but once Ron D heard the nigga Dogg say Bella's name, he knew that he had to hit Mo up. There was no other chick in the hood with the name Bella. Ron D figured that something wasn't right.

Chapter 17

Staten Island

"This house is beautiful. Mom, did you see the patio. It is a pure delight," Andrea said cheerfully.

"Yes. I don't know how we got this house, but I love it. Your father said there will be a driver here shortly that will take us to the mall to pick out some things for the house. I haven't been shopping in so long," Evelyn admitted.

"I'm glad you're feeling so much better mom. I don't know why you hid the fact that you were able to speak from me. I'm just glad that you're back to feeling like yourself again. Do you think you will be able to go back to the doctor to make sure that you're getting better?" Andrea questioned.

"I have no choice. Your father wouldn't hear of me not going to see about my health issues. He said that he will take me himself to the doctor next week. I'm praying for a positive report. I have to call my sister. I can't imagine what she's going through right now."

Evelyn didn't like that her family was coming together and things were looking up for her while Sheryl had just lost her son and going through turmoil.

"I think Aunt Sheryl would be ecstatic to hear how good you're talking and would temporarily take her mind off of her grieving. This is what she has been praying for and I know it would brighten up her day if she heard from you," Andrea mentioned. Evelyn smiled, knowing that her sister would be surprised to know how well she'd been doing.

"Give me your phone. I'm going to call her now," Evelyn said.

***

Basement

Mo, Gus, Josiah, Rabbit, Taz, and Po sat downstairs in the basement of the house discussing plans. Mo sat back as he watched his father take over everything. T Ski had given him the same details but was surprised when his father had instructed them on a few projects that hadn't been discussed with Mo. Mo was excited about his pop being home, but he didn't like the fact that he was coming home trying to run things. He had his life turned upside down because of T Ski and now it seemed like T Ski was shitting on him.

Mo didn't know if he was really mad or just a bit jealous that he wasn't in charge. Taz was even sitting in the meeting and he had vowed that he wasn't going to be involved. Mo knew that everyone was going to start changing around him now that his father was home. If Po was going to be running things, this was a good time for Mo to get his life on track and move on.

"Rabbit, I need you to get Gulley on the phone and let him know that we need him and his crazy ass brother. These young cats don't know what it takes to run a successful business on the streets. We not new to this shit. The rules of the street don't change. This idea is genius and it will make us all a shit load of money to get the hell out of NY for good. I know I'm not going back to jail and I'm sure no man sitting at this table are going. We need this shit to be extra tight and we have to watch each other's back," Po explained. Everyone was in agreement and continued to listen as Po began to tell them the game plan that T Ski had put together.

Mo's phone beeped, alerting him that someone had left him a text message. Mo grabbed his phone from his pocket and saw 911 pop up on the screen from Ron D's number. Mo stood from his seat and walked away out of ear range so the other guys wouldn't hear his conversation. Mo dialed Ron D's number and waited for him to answer.

"Yo. Son, I got some shit to tell you. I just left from checking my cousin Ace. This nigga introduced me to a nigga name Dogg. This nigga got a hold to some info he said from your baby moms. This nigga is stupid, my nigga. He shot me the whole rundown to his plans and don't know shit about me or who I rock with. He made a copycat of the K2O shit and is putting it out on the streets. This nigga is about to have a war on his hand because he done gave DC's people some next shit and they will be after him in a minute. He's trying to build his own team to go up against them niggas so he can take over their turf."

Mo listened intently to the words that came from Ron D's mouth. Mo could feel his anger arising. Bella was truly showing him a different side of her. He didn't know how she got the ingredients when T Ski was the only one that knew of it.

"This shit is crazy. She hit my phone up earlier, telling me she was at my crib. I didn't speak with her or hit her back. Yo, thanks for the info. Are you trying to link up with these niggas?" Mo questioned. He had to make sure that no heat came his friend's way. He hoped that Ron D wouldn't associate himself with them but Mo couldn't tell a grown man what to do.

"I took a few pieces from those niggas to see what it look like but you already know, bro, I don't fuck with lames. I will hold this shit for you so you can check it out for yourself," Ron D replied.

"Good looking. I'm gon' hit you back in a minute. I'll let you know what's good then," Mo said as he disconnected the call.

Mo sent a text to T Ski letting him know everything Ron D had shared with him including what was told to him about Bella. He knew that she couldn't be trusted. All he had done for her and she still betrayed him. Mo couldn't think of anyone she could've gotten information from. He remembered when he went to speak to Bella in the hospital and how she bashed his family, calling them all names. Mo was trying to put two and two together but couldn't bring himself to believe that anyone from his family would tell her a thing.

"Mo, what are you doing?" Po shouted.

"I'm right here," Mo said as he headed back to sit in with the guys.

"I was just telling them that we're going to meet up with all the hitters from out of town. We need to introduce ourselves and let them know that we are the guys they will be reporting to from here on out. I heard that this nigga name DC is one of our problems along with Syracuse from the 90s. He got down there on lock, along with Prospect Plaza. They crew is tight and on point. We have to move with force and make sure that we clean that shit up quickly. Time isn't on our side. We need to really dominate Brownsville and take this shit up a notch."

Mo listened to his father along with the others. Mo was waiting to hear back from T Ski. He wanted to know what the next move would be. He wasn't about to tell his father what he was told. Mo felt obligated to keep that to himself until he got back word from T Ski on what to do next.

***

Langston Hughes

"What the fuck are you calling me for, Panama? You know I am out here handling business. This shit can wait until I get back to Brooklyn," DC snapped.

"Nah, this couldn't wait. We have a big problem," Panama stated.

"What the fuck do you mean we have a big problem? Nigga, I only been gone from the block for a few hours. What the fuck could've possibly gone wrong in such a short time?" DC ranted.

"Cali and Drew was found dead today. Both shot in the head while sitting on the bench. Niggas didn't see shit. I don't know who the fuck would come at our people and that's the fucked up part about it. Those out of town niggas are only looking to knock off the heads. Word is that Tadow left BK and we know he didn't know who smoked his brother. That's not all, though. Jason got pressed by some of those out of towners. Shit about to go haywire, son," Panama remarked.

"What the fuck, yo? Out of all the days that I was there, shit gets out of hand once I leave. This is some bullshit. I can't get back out there right now. You will need to handle this, Panama. If these niggas ready to rumble, get our niggas on the phone and tell them it's time to show face. I don't want to hear back from you with no bad news," DC stated angrily and ended the call.

Panama shook his head. He knew that he had to fix this shit and fast before reporting back to DC. It was time for him to get shit popping.

***

T Ski read the message Mo had sent him. He shook his head at the thought of some lame ass niggas trying to copycat his product. There was no way Bella could give anyone the ingredients to put together what he created. Something didn't sit right with T Ski. He didn't have time for this.

"What's wrong T?" Kya asked.

"I just received a text from my brother. Some guys in the hood are trying to copycat K2O. They don't know what they're doing and could possibly kill people, depending on what they have mixed together. My brother's baby mother has been going around giving information to her ex-boyfriend but she doesn't know what's mixed in K2O. I need to get my people out there to handle this. I was hoping that we could get to the airport a little early but it doesn't seem like that's going to happen right now." T Ski was annoyed as he pulled out his phone and sent out mass text messages to a few of his people.

"T, I told you that it would be fine if you didn't fly out with me. You could always meet me down there. You need to handle this. It's not good business for your men if someone else is out there duplicating K2O and people wind up getting sick behind it. Everyone is going to lose out because I'm sure people would go looking out of BK to get their next fix if this isn't handled," Kya shared.

T Ski shook his head. He knew that Kya was right and he was already getting things in motion. He was not letting his future wife fly alone, even though he had five of his men flying out there alongside her. It wasn't the same as him being there himself.

"I got this covered. I need to go out for a minute but I'll be back in an hour top. Be ready to leave when I get back." Kya smiled as T Ski proceeded out of the house.

T Ski made it out of the building. Pablo was sitting in the car when he noticed T Ski. He hurried to get out of the car, heading toward the side walk so he could open the door for T Ski. He entered the vehicle and pulled out his lap top. T Ski was about to get to the bottom of this. Appearing on the screen was a big picture of Brownsville. T Ski zoomed in to see what was going on. He could see that the crime unit was out in Seth Low Projects, most likely investigating Drew and Cali's murders. T Ski then zoomed in on Langston Hughes. He saw a dude talking on the phone and looked tense. T Ski pulled out his headphones and plugged them into the side of the laptop. He typed in a few words and waited until connected flashed at the bottom of the screen.

T Ski overheard Panama talking to DC over the phone. T Ski had to make a move now. He pulled the headphones from his ear and sent a text to Mo. T Ski was pushing for time and didn't want to spend much of it worrying about this problem. T Ski then hit up his team and told them that shit was about to go down. He needed everyone on their p's and q's. He would hit them back with more details.

"Fuck," T Ski shouted. He didn't have much time to wait on Mo and his pops to make it to Brownsville, being that they were at the house all the way in Staten Island. T Ski had to handle this himself. "Pablo, I need you to swing by and pick up Mecca." T Ski sent a text to Mecca's phone and told him to be ready. T Ski looked at his watch and knew that it might be impossible for him to make it back to Kya to escort her to Atlanta. He didn't want to disappoint her but he didn't see making it on time. This angered him. Shit was about to get turned all the way up.

***

Pablo had reached the front of the tan colored business that was fourteen stories high. Mecca was waiting out front, standing next to the curb. Mecca entered the vehicle and knew that shit was about to go down from the look on T Ski's face.

"What's good?" Mecca asked, once securely inside the car.

"We have to get rid of DC's people right now. Shit is popping off on the other side so we have to be careful. Cops is out tight right now, but these motherfuckers trying to come at our people so we have to get at them first. DC's right hand man, Panama, is calling all the shots. I got his location and trailing the nigga but they have people all over so we have to play this shit cool. I already sent out word for the boys to be on a lookout. Get Joey and Beans on the line and tell them I need them and they're boys to be at Langston Hughes in fifteen minutes. Get Baker and his boys to cover their turf until we handle business."

T Ski pulled open his laptop again and typed a few things, pulling up a new screen. He had a location for some of DC's top dogs and those were the first on his list to hit up. T Ski kept checking his time. He decided to send Kya a text.

T Ski told her to meet him at the airport in three hours. He knew she wanted to get there early but they were going to have to take a later flight. He wasn't letting her go alone and that was final. T Ski knew she would probably be upset because she wanted to make it there in good timing so they could check out a few places before it got too late. They were going to do that tomorrow because T Ski had to handle his business first.

Sonovia Alexander

Chapter 18

Langston Hughes

"Yo, we about to set shit off on those out of town niggas. Niggas is starting to fuck with our people and these niggas need to know that they not running shit over here. Meet me at the crib in ten minutes. Link up with Shabazz and let him know it's time to put in some work. I don't give a fuck who's out there. Niggas better blast at any of them niggas that look suspect," Panama ordered.

"We heading out right now. I'll hit Shabazz jack and let him know to meet up with us. It shouldn't be no police over there since they got shit locked down on Seth Low," Lance stated.

"I know. Since niggas are getting pressed by these out of towners, it's time that we show these niggas that we aren't to be fucked with. Make sure shit is good over there before you head this way. Business still has to go on," Panama said.

"I'm on it. We'll be there in ten minutes top," Lance said before ending the call.

Panama grabbed his .357 revolver and tucked it in the back of his pants. Panama checked his watch and saw that it was 4:52 p.m. Panama waited anxiously for his team of men to get to him. He knew that he wouldn't be able to call DC with bad news.

Panama had to hold shit down while DC was away. He had to show and prove himself. DC was on his way to retirement and Panama had to show him that he could still hold shit down while he wasn't present. Panama was next in line to take over the hood and he had been waiting a long time for this to happen. He wasn't about to let no one get what he felt was rightfully his. He earned it and was going to make sure that he made it to the top.

Although he was making good money, he could gross a quarter of a million dollars more than he was making now working under DC. Panama was thirty-four years old and didn't have nothing to lose. He didn't have kids, he wasn't married, and didn't even have a steady woman by his side. Panama was too busy chasing a dream. He wanted to be the top dog and he had put in enough work over the years for DC to get to that point. Panama was putting his squad to the test to see who was ride or dies. He was going to take mental notes on how they moved to see who qualified to run side by side with him. He had called all of DC's top captains to take these niggas down. Panama was certain that he had chosen the right niggas to take with him. He was ready to set shit off and let niggas know that he was nothing to be fucked with.

***

T Ski removed his gold watch and replaced it with another watch. Mecca looked over, wondering why he was switching watches at a time like this.

"Nigga, I know you're not trying to be stylish when we're about to go get our hands dirty," Mecca remarked. T Ski chuckled.

"This is an iP1-Pistole with iW1 active RFID watch," T Ski responded.

"What the fuck does that mean?" Mecca questioned. T Ski pulled out a pretty silver gun that piqued Mecca's interest.

"This is an Armatix iP1 pistol. The only way it can work the way it needs to be is if I have the watch on," T Ski explained.

"Where the fuck you get that shit from? That shit is hot," Mecca exclaimed.

"I got some shit man. There's Joey and Beans. It's time to get to work," T Ski added, changing the topic. It was no time for him to be sitting around explaining to Mecca about his gun. They had to move quickly.

"What's good? I'm Kane. We are heading up to the 5th floor. I'll move in first and you niggas just hold me down," T Ski said to the guys. They nodded in agreement. Joey had never met T Ski and was absent to the fact that he was working for a teenager. Mecca gave Beans and Joey dap before following T Ski into the building.

"Where are your guys positioned at?" Mecca asked Joey once inside the building.

"They are posted up. They're watching. We got this," Joey stated.

Mecca shook his head as they all took the staircase leading up to the fifth floor.

When the guys reached the floor, T Ski took the lead and searched for the apartment number he needed. T Ski pulled out a pendant he had in his pocket and picked the lock. When he heard the click sound, he pulled out his pistol while entering the apartment. Mecca, Joey, and Beans had their guns drawn as they followed behind T Ski. T Ski moved toward the living room and posted up against the wall. He peeked his head around the corner to see where Panama was positioned in hopes not to get caught. Panama was standing by the window looking out for his boys.

T Ski placed his finger to his lips letting the guys know to be quiet. He peeked his head around the corner once again before he entered the living room. T Ski fired one shot, hitting Panama in the back. Blood splattered on the blinds as Panama fell against the window, grimacing in pain. T Ski moved in a little closer and aimed for Panama's head. He let off a single shot, killing Panama instantly. T Ski checked for Panama's phone, finding it in the side of his pocket. T Ski placed the phone into his pocket and walked out of the living room, heading for the front door. T Ski opened the door and proceeded toward the staircase with his guys following closely behind.

Panama's phone started going off. T Ski pulled it from his pocket as he continued down the stairs. T Ski pressed the talk button. He didn't say anything.

"We coming close to the building now. Meet us downstairs," Lance said. T Ski ended the call. He grabbed his gun from behind his back and held it in his hand.

"You said your boys was posted up, right?" T Ski yelled over his shoulder.

"Yea," Joey replied.

"These niggas shouldn't make it inside the building." T Ski shook his head hoping that these guys were ready to start taking niggas' heads off.

T Ski was the first to reach the outside of the building. He could see Panama's guys walking up the crosswalk. T Ski moved toward the side of the building. Mecca, Joey, and Beans followed suit, seeing the guys at the same time. Joey looked across toward the next building and made eye contact with one of his guys. He signaled, showing their targets coming up the walkway. Before Lance and the other seven men reached the door, T Ski was the first to let off shots in their direction, hitting one of the guys. Shots started being fired from across the building all targeting the same men. Guys ran from the back and started letting off shots in the direction of Lance and his boys. T Ski started running toward the car with Mecca following closely behind. Pablo already had the car cranked and ready. T Ski was proud to see that his guys were down for whatever. He didn't move until he saw all of Panama's guys down.

T Ski had to get out of there before someone noticed who he was. Once he and Mecca were safely inside the car, Pablo pulled off, driving at normal speed. T Ski put his gun away and removed the watch from his wrist. T Ski pulled out his cell phone and sent a text to Joey. He told them to head to the hotel and lay low for the remainder of the day. T Ski didn't think it would be that easy and quick to knock all those guys off. He underestimated the crew he had under him.

T Ski had one less thing to worry about but knew that it was far from over. DC was going to get word sooner or later about his men and was going to be ready for war. He knew that his pops and Mo would be able to handle that when the time came. T Ski had caught his first body at the age of fourteen. It was like he lived a whole other life outside of his family. T Ski had killed one of the men that tried to test him, thinking that he was weak.

Dude didn't see it coming. T Ski had gotten ahold of a .45 and blew dude's head off. T Ski had started recruiting men at that time and was taken as a joke. He knew that he was going to run into problems like this, especially with men that had pride. No man wanted to be caught dead working for a boy that they felt hadn't even hit puberty yet. They would soon learn that T Ski wasn't their ordinary fourteen year old.

"I need to hit Kya up and let her know that I'll be there sooner than later. I need you to meet up with my brother and let him know what has gone down. He has some shit that he needs to put you on to that he found out today. I need to get on this flight and see Kya off to school. I don't think I'll be able to stay as long as planned. I just need to make sure that she gets there safely and settles in before heading back out. I'm gon' drop you at the crib and you need to get on that now. Shit is going to get hot and our men need to be ready at all times," T Ski riposte.

"I got you," Mecca replied. He was grateful to T Ski for all that he did for his niece. He hoped they could enjoy their lives together and be happy because they truly deserved it. Mecca cleaned off his gun before putting it back in the small of his back. He leaned his head back in the seat and rested his eyes.

Chapter 19

Mo had received a text message asking him to meet in Brooklyn stat. T Ski had informed him that he would be working side by side with Mecca. T Ski said that he knew the operation just as he. Mo replied back to the text and told Mecca that he would be on his way. Mo had his own personal reasons why he wanted to head to Brooklyn. His father had ended the meeting a few minutes ago. His mother, sister, and son were out shopping with a few security. Po, Josiah, and Rabbit had gone to meet up with a few people.

Mo had taken a nice, long, hot shower. He tossed on a red tee with some black khaki shorts. It was hot outside. Mo went through the house inspecting it and was pleased with T Ski's taste. The house had a full basement, five bedrooms, a den, living and dining room, three full bathrooms and a spacious kitchen. The attic wasn't that big, but was big enough.

Mo couldn't see himself getting comfortable here. Although the house was beautiful, it belonged to his parents. Mo had plans of his own to get something nice for him and Xavier. He had to be his own man and take care of himself along with his son.

Mo sat on the bed in the room that he and Xavier were sharing. The house was fully decorated. Mo thought about what his son would think of him if he knew the life he was living. Mo had so many dreams for his son. Any man would want their child to be a better man than they had been. Mo was proud to be a father and thought that he would bring his son up in a two parent home. Something that he had been cheated out of. That was the reason for Mo getting his life straight and getting a good job to be a provider. He had seen back then that he was following in his father's footsteps. That wasn't the man Mo wanted to be.

Mo laid back on the bed and enjoyed the peace and quiet. It made him reflect back over his life. He wondered where he had gone wrong with Bella. She was the only woman he had been in love with. He couldn't help but still love her even after finding out about her betrayal and cheating. For the sake of their son, Mo hoped that one day they would be able to save their relationship and start over. Mo couldn't see himself being with her at this moment.

He knew that he had to speak to Bella. He needed to know who had given her the drop on T Ski's operation. She didn't know much to go on because Mo had never told her too much. The only person Mo could think of was Taz B. Mo didn't believe that Taz would share that kind of information with Bella willingly.

Mo's mind was in overdrive, trying to figure out things and how they had spiraled out of control like this. Taz was downstairs in the basement. Mo was contemplating on whether or not he wanted to approach him about the situation. Mo kept coming up empty for any of the possible suspects that would've spoken to Bella. He couldn't think of no other person other than Taz. Taz was obviously not down with T Ski's plans from the start but Mo still didn't know what Taz would gain by telling Bella about K2O. He didn't have one hundred percent of the facts to go on and neither did anyone else concerning K2O.

Mo jumped up from the bed when his cell phone started vibrating in his pocket. It startled him. He reached for his phone and looked at the caller ID. He notice it was Bella calling. He was about to ignore the call but decided to answer.

"Yo," Mo said into the phone.

"Mo, I have been trying to reach you. I need to see you. There is so much I need to say to you and I know that you're going to be upset, but I need to talk to you face to face," Bella blurted out. She wanted to get her words out before he hung up on her.

"Where are you?" Mo questioned.

"I'm staying with my friend, Nancy," Bella replied.

"I know where she's at. I'll be over there to see you in about an hour and a half," Mo remarked.

"How's Xavier? Are you going to bring my son to see me?" Bella asked.

"Not until after we talk. I'll see you soon." Mo didn't wait for a response before he disconnected the call. Mo got up from the bed and headed out of the bedroom. He walked down the long hallway heading for the stairs. Mo had always imagined living in a big beautiful house like this. He thought that it would be Bella and Xavier's dream to live like this. Those were dreams Mo had once upon a time.

Mo descended the stairs to the basement in search of Taz B. Taz B sat at the table going over some documents he had in front of him.

"Yo, I need to ask you something while we're alone," Mo said as he stood over Taz.

"What's up?" Taz said, keeping his eyes fixed on the documents.

"I need you to be honest with me, bro. This is important. Did you give Bella any information about K2O?" Mo questioned.

Taz B dropped the pen he had in his hand and stared up at his brother.

"Make this your last time that you fucking question me about doing some foul shit. Why the fuck would I give her information about something I don't have the full details to? That's your fucking girl, not mine. Why the fuck you think I would talk to her about something that I didn't even want parts of? Mo, stop bringing this shit to me. I don't accept the shit you and T Ski got going on and still don't want any parts of it, but I would never cross my brothers for no one," Taz B spat angrily.

"Listen, calm the fuck down. You are the only person that could've told her anything and that's why I brought it to your attention. Some shit is going down because of Bella. Somehow she got wind of K2O and she gave the information to a nigga she's been fucking with named Dogg. He made a duplicate of the product and is selling the shit in the hood," Mo explained.

Taz B raised a brow in surprise after hearing Mo's confession.

"How the fuck was she able to provide anyone with information unless T Ski gave her the info himself, and we already know that's not possible. That's puzzling. How did you find this out?" Taz questioned.

"The stupid motherfucker sang like a bird, telling Ron D everything so he could join their team and push the work for them, as well as take over DC turf," Mo explained.

"Did you tell pop?" Taz asked.

"No. I wanted to wait until after I spoke to T Ski."

Taz saw the change in Mo's facial expression along with his voice. He could tell that his brother wasn't fond of the idea of their father coming home after all these years trying to take over. Mo wasn't fooling anyone. Taz knew that his brother loved his father but Mo had been the man in charge for the last few years. He wasn't ready to give the title back to his pop as being the man of the house. Taz could feel it and see it in Mo's eyes.

"What did T Ski say about it?" Taz asked.

"He told me he was going to get to the bottom of it. I'll be back. I'm going to see Bella," Mo said before heading toward the stairs.

Chapter 20

Bedford Stuyvesant
Halsey Street

"Are you okay, girl?" Nancy asked Bella.

"Hell no I'm not okay. This nigga is on his way here and I'm afraid he might want to beat my ass after he finds out what I've done. I don't think I have enough heart to tell him," Bella admitted.

"Honey, I know you're scared but you have done enough damage. No sense in continuing to lie. Just tell him everything and get it all out. Shit, you need that nigga," Nancy said.

"I want to be with him and I know that if I tell him everything, Nancy, we will never get back together. I don't know if I'll be able to deal with being without him. Our son would love to have us all back together as a family. I just don't know what else to do right now. I love him and I know he's going to be torn. I don't want to hurt him anymore." Bella wiped a single tear that fell from her eyes. She was literally afraid of facing Mo. She had a feeling that things weren't going to turn out well for her once they finally spoke.

"I know you don't sweetie, but you can't go on living with these lies. You have no choice but to reveal everything, knowing that your crazy ex is still out there. Brooklyn isn't that big. You will be bound to run into that nigga again and if you don't tell Mo everything, he would never know that you need his protection. No matter how bad things may seem, tell him everything. You owe him that much and you owe it to your son. How can you live your life in fear with a kid? That's not going to be healthy for either of you," Nancy retorted.

"I know and you're right. I guess I don't have a choice but to tell him the truth. I need for you to stay in here with me just in case this nigga tries to kill me," Bella said seriously.

"Mo loves you too much to hurt you. You will be just fine, but I will stick around for moral support," Nancy remarked.

"Thanks." Bella walked over to the mirror to check herself out. She was wearing a one piece denim Guess dress that was a halter cut and stopped above her thigh. She had on her wedges. Her hair was combed down with a center part. Bella checked her make-up and was pleased with her looks. She went to the bathroom for a release. She was still nervous about seeing Mo.

A half hour had gone by before Mo knocked on the door. Bella was seated in the kitchen looking out the window while

Nancy was watching television. Bella walked slowly over to the door. She unlocked it and opened it wide. Mo didn't look like he was happy to see her.

"Hey," Bella spoke.

"What up?" Mo replied.

"Come inside," Bella offered. Mo stepped past her inside of the apartment. Mo stood by the door. "Let's go inside the kitchen and talk," Bella said as she entered the kitchen. Mo followed behind her and sat down at the table.

"How long have you been fucking this dude?" Mo didn't beat around the bush. He got straight to the point. He didn't have long to talk and had to be leaving soon. He wanted to get the answers he needed before he was on his way.

"I haven't fucked Dogg in years. I fucked him once out of fear two months before I got pregnant with Xavier. That was the last time I swear."

Mo tried his best to contain his anger. He wanted to knock her out.

"You fucked this nigga raw dog and was fucking me too?" Mo said as he screwed his face up at Bella.

"I never fucked him raw, Mo," Bella admitted.

"How the fuck could you tell another man that my son belongs to him. Is there something you need to tell me about Xavier's paternity?" Mo knew it was his son but he wanted confirmation from Bella.

"I told you I was afraid of Dogg. He was upset that he didn't have that same control over me that he used to when we were together. He kept showing up to the house and, like I said, you weren't there to protect me and I was scared of him. He used to get physical and I just didn't want to go through that with him. I had told him that Xavier was his son so he wouldn't beat me up the day he cornered me. He wanted me to help him get to the top. He knew that I had friends that were making a lot of money and he just wanted to get put on," Bella explained.

"So you told him what my brother had planned to get this nigga to the top. What the fuck is wrong with you? If a nigga was trying to blackmail your ass or get you to do something that you didn't want to do, why you didn't tell me. You know I would've taken care of that problem to make sure that you were good," Mo confessed.

"I wanted to tell you but I was embarrassed. He was some dirty ass knucklehead that don't have shit still trying to come for me and I didn't know how to tell you that without being ashamed for some of the things that I did while being with him," Bella admitted.

"I don't give a fuck about your past Bella and you knew that. I loved you for who you were and who you were becoming. That's all bullshit excuses that don't hold no weight. I need to know something though," Mo said.

"What's that?" Bella didn't know what else Mo wanted to know but she was glad that she was getting everything out in the open. She hoped that he didn't ask her for specific details because she wasn't going there with him.

"How the fuck were you able to give this motherfucker information about K2O if no one knew what was mixed in it but T Ski," Mo asked.

"T Ski wasn't the only one that knew what he was mixing up," Bella added.

"What the fuck do you mean by that? I know there was no one else at my crib that would've given you that kind of information. I already hit up Taz and he said he didn't give it to you. T Ski definitely wouldn't have told you. I didn't fill you in on much, so I want to know how you figured this shit out," Mo said, raising his voice.

"You forgot about the one person T Ski had a close relationship with."

Mo rolled his eyes in the air. "Bella, I don't have all fucking day. Tell me how the fuck did you know what to tell this motherfucker about my brother's product. Stop beating around the bush because I don't play those guessing games. Tell me everything I need to know now while you have the chance," Mo was getting annoyed.

"Xavier told me," Bella admitted.

Mo's eyes grew wide as he looked at Bella with disbelief. His son couldn't have. Mo stopped and thought, and shook his head.

"No," was all Mo could manage to say.

To be continued...
Brooklyn on Lock 3
Coming Soon

Coming Soon From Lock Down Publications

RESTRAINING ORDER

By **CA$H & COFFEE**

GANGSTA CITY **II**

By **Teddy Duke**

A DANGEROUS LOVE **VII**

By **J Peach**

BLOOD OF A BOSS **III**

By **Askari**

THE KING CARTEL **III**

By **Frank Gresham**

NEVER TRUST A RATCHET BITCH

SILVER PLATTER HOE **III**

By **Reds Johnson**

THESE NIGGAS AIN'T LOYAL **III**

By **Nikki Tee**

BROOKLYN ON LOCK **III**

By **Sonovia Alexander**

THE STREETS BLEED MURDER **II**

By **Jerry Jackson**

CONFESSIONS OF A DOPEMAN'S DAUGHTER **II**

By **Rasstrina**

WHAT ABOUT US **II**

NEVER LOVE AGAIN

By **Kim Kaye**

Sonovia Alexander

A GANGSTER'S REVENGE

By **Aryanna**

Available Now

LOVE KNOWS NO BOUNDARIES **I II & III**

By **Coffee**

SILVER PLATTER HOE **I & II**

HONEY DIPP **I & II**

CLOSED LEGS DON'T GET FED **I & II**

A BITCH NAMED KARMA

By **Reds Johnson**

A DANGEROUS LOVE **I, II, III, IV, V, VI**

By **J Peach**

CUM FOR ME

An **LDP Erotica Collaboration**

THE KING CARTEL **I & II**

By **Frank Gresham**

BLOOD OF A BOSS **I & II**

By **Askari**

THE DEVIL WEARS TIMBS

BURY ME A G **I II & III**

By **Tranay Adams**

THESE NIGGAS AIN'T LOYAL **I & II**

By **Nikki Tee**

THE STREETS BLEED MURDER

By **Jerry Jackson**

DIRTY LICKS

By **Peter Mack**

THE ULTIMATE BETRAYAL

By **Phoenix**

BROOKLYN ON LOCK

By **Sonovia Alexander**

SLEEPING IN HEAVEN, WAKING IN HELL **I, II & III**

By **Forever Redd**

THE DEVIL WEARS TIMBS **I, II & III**

By **Tranay Adams**

DON'T FU#K WITH MY HEART **I & II**

By **Linnea**

BOSS'N UP **I & II**

By **Royal Nicole**

LOYALTY IS BLIND

By **Kenneth Chisholm**

<u>BOOKS BY LDP'S CEO, CA$H</u>

TRUST NO MAN
TRUST NO MAN 2
TRUST NO MAN 3
BONDED BY BLOOD
SHORTY GOT A THUG
A DIRTY SOUTH LOVE
THUGS CRY
THUGS CRY 2
TRUST NO BITCH
TRUST NO BITCH 2
TRUST NO BITCH 3
TIL MY CASKET DROPS

Coming Soon

TRUST NO BITCH (KIAM EYEZ' STORY)
THUGS CRY 3
BONDED BY BLOOD 2
RESTRANING ORDER

Sonovia Alexander

Made in the USA
Middletown, DE
27 July 2024